PRAISE FOR TONI MORRISON'S

God Help the Child

"Magnificent. . . . Morrison remains an incredibly powerful writer who commands attention no matter the story she is telling."　　　　　　　*—The Guardian* (London)

"Sly, savage, honest, and elegant. . . . Once again, Morrison thrillingly brings the storytelling moxie and mojo that make her, arguably, our greatest living novelist."　*—Elle*

"Exquisite. . . . Morrison has a Shakespearean sense of tragedy, and that gift imbues *God Help the Child*."　*—Newsday*

"The Nobel Prize winner continues to create beauty from the anger and defining wounds of her characters. . . . Bears a lifetime's worth of anger and sorrow, distilled to their essences and fiercely hung on to, tooth and claw."
—The Christian Science Monitor

"Glorious and incendiary."　　*—The Philadelphia Inquirer*

"There is a new urgency to Morrison's work, a desire to tell the story itself, without embellishment or ornamentation. . . . Morrison [is] the undisputed interpreter of the American black experience."　　*—The Boston Globe*

"Morrison gives us an unflinching look at the wounds that adults can inflict on children with life-altering consequences. . . . Few authors can deliver exquisitely written prose as Morrison."   —Essence.com

"Haunting. . . . Moving. . . . Fearless. . . . *God Help the Child* yet again proves that Toni Morrison is an icon." —*Bustle*

"Both timely and timeless. . . . A pleasure. . . . As she shows with such brevity and eloquence in *God Help the Child*, having and healing don't necessarily happen at the same time."   —*The Seattle Times*

"A book to be read twice at a minimum—the first time for the story, and the second time to savor the language, the gems of phrasing and the uncomfortable revelations about the human capacity both to love and destroy."
—*Pittsburgh Post-Gazette*

"Breathtaking prose. . . . A new Morrison book is always cause for celebration."   —*The Dallas Morning News*

"We have stepped into, once again, another of Morrison's fertile landscapes. . . . It is a blessing that she still speaks with such salvific force and poetic grace."   —*The Plain Dealer*

"Heartbreaking. . . . [Morrison] continues to dazzle. . . . Morrison—like Bride—is still reinventing herself as a writer. And just getting better." —*St. Louis Post-Dispatch*

TONI MORRISON

God Help the Child

Toni Morrison is the author of eleven novels, from *The Bluest Eye* (1970) to *God Help the Child* (2015). She received the National Book Critics Circle Award, the Pulitzer Prize, and in 1993 she was awarded the Nobel Prize in Literature. She died in 2019.

INTERNATIONAL

ALSO BY TONI MORRISON

God Help the Child

God Help the Child

❧

A Novel

TONI MORRISON

VINTAGE INTERNATIONAL
Vintage Books
A Division of Penguin Random House LLC
New York

Grateful acknowledgment is made to SA Music LLC and Hal Leonard Corporation for permission to reprint an excerpt from "Stormy Weather," lyrics by Ted Koehler and music by Harold Arlen, copyright © 1933, copyright renewed © 1961 by Fred Ahlert Music Group (ASCAP) and Ted Koehler Music Co. (ASCAP) and SA Music LLC. Fred Ahlert Music Group (ASCAP) and Ted Koehler Music Co. (ASCAP) administered by Bug Music, Inc., a BMG Chrysalis Company. All rights reserved. Reprinted by permission of SA Music LLC and Hal Leonard Corporation.

The Library of Congress has cataloged the Knopf edition as follows:
Morrison, Toni.
God help the child / Toni Morrison. — First edition.
pages ; cm
1. African Americans—Fiction.
2. Mothers and daughters—Fiction.   I. Title.
PS3563.O8749G63 2015   813'.54—DC23   2014034972

Vintage International Trade Paperback ISBN: 978-0-307-74092-2
eBook ISBN: 978-0-385-35317-5

Book design by Cassandra J. Pappas

www.vintagebooks.com

Printed in the United States of America
14   16   18   20   22   21   19   17   15   13

For You

Suffer little children to come unto me,
and forbid them not

LUKE 18:16

PART I

Sweetness

It's not my fault. So you can't blame me. I didn't do it and have no idea how it happened. It didn't take more than an hour after they pulled her out from between my legs to realize something was wrong. Really wrong. She was so black she scared me. Midnight black, Sudanese black. I'm light-skinned, with good hair, what we call high yellow, and so is Lula Ann's father. Ain't nobody in my family anywhere near that color. Tar is the closest I can think of yet her hair don't go with the skin. It's different—straight but curly like those naked tribes in Australia. You might think she's a throwback, but throwback to what? You should've seen my grandmother; she passed for white and never said another word to any one of her children. Any letter she got from my mother or my aunts she sent right back, unopened. Finally they got the message of no message and let her be. Almost all mulatto types and quadroons did that back in the day— if they had the right kind of hair, that is. Can you imagine how many white folks have Negro blood running and hiding in their veins? Guess. Twenty percent, I heard. My own mother, Lula Mae, could have passed easy, but she chose not to. She told me the price she paid for that decision. When she and my father went to the courthouse to get married there were two Bibles and they had to put their hands on the one reserved for Negroes. The other one was for white people's hands. The Bible! Can you beat it? My mother was housekeeper for a rich white couple. They ate every meal she cooked and insisted she scrub their backs while they sat in the tub and God knows what other intimate things they made her do, but no touching of the same Bible.

Some of you probably think it's a bad thing to group ourselves according to skin color—the lighter, the better—in social clubs, neighborhoods, churches, sororities, even colored schools. But how else can we hold on to a little dignity? How else can you avoid being spit on in a drugstore, shoving elbows at the bus stop, walking in the gutter to let whites have the whole sidewalk, charged a nickel at the grocer's for a paper bag that's free to white shoppers? Let alone all the name-calling. I heard about all of that and much, much more. But because of my mother's skin color, she wasn't stopped from trying on hats in the department stores or using their ladies' room. And my father could try on shoes in the front part of the shoestore, not in a back room. Neither one would let themselves drink from a "colored only" fountain even if they were dying of thirst.

I hate to say it, but from the very beginning in the maternity ward the baby, Lula Ann, embarrassed me. Her birth skin was pale like all babies', even African ones, but it changed fast. I thought I was going crazy when she turned blue-black right before my eyes. I know I went crazy for a minute because once—just for a few seconds—I held a blanket over her face and pressed. But I couldn't do that, no matter how much I wished she hadn't been born with that terrible color. I even thought of giving her away to an orphanage someplace. And I was scared to be one of those mothers who put their babies on church steps. Recently I heard about a couple in Germany, white as snow, who had a dark-skinned baby nobody could explain. Twins, I believe—one white, one colored. But I don't know if it's true. All I know is that for me, nursing her was like having a pickaninny sucking my teat. I went to bottle-feeding soon as I got home.

My husband, Louis, is a porter and when he got back off the rails he looked at me like I really was crazy and looked at her like she was from the planet Jupiter. He wasn't a cussing man so when he said, "Goddamn! What the hell is this?" I knew we were in trouble. That's what did it—what caused the fights between me and him. It broke our marriage to pieces. We had three good years together but when she was born he blamed me and treated Lula Ann like she was a stranger—more than that, an enemy.

He never touched her. I never did convince him that I ain't never, ever fooled around with another man. He was dead sure I was lying. We argued and argued till I told him her blackness must be from his own family—not mine. That's when it got worse, so bad he just up and left and I had to look for another, cheaper place to live. I knew enough not to take her with me when I applied to landlords so I left her with a teenage cousin to babysit. I did the best I could and didn't take her outside much anyway because when I pushed her in the baby carriage, friends or strangers would lean down and peek in to say something nice and then give a start or jump back before frowning. That hurt. I could have been the babysitter if our skin colors were reversed. It was hard enough just being a colored woman—even a high-yellow one—trying to rent in a decent part of the city. Back in the nineties when Lula Ann was born, the law was against discriminating in who you could rent to, but not many landlords paid attention to it. They made up reasons to keep you out. But I got lucky with Mr. Leigh. I know he upped the rent seven dollars from what he advertised, and he has a fit if you a minute late with the money.

I told her to call me "Sweetness" instead of "Mother" or "Mama." It was safer. Being that black and having what I think are too-thick lips calling me "Mama" would confuse people. Besides, she has funny-colored eyes, crow-black with a blue tint, something witchy about them too.

So it was just us two for a long while and I don't have to tell you how hard it is being an abandoned wife. I guess

Louis felt a little bit bad after leaving us like that because a few months later on he found out where I moved to and started sending me money once a month, though I never asked him to and didn't go to court to get it. His fifty-dollar money orders and my night job at the hospital got me and Lula Ann off welfare. Which was a good thing. I wish they would stop calling it welfare and go back to the word they used when my mother was a girl. Then it was called "Relief." Sounds much better, like it's just a short-term breather while you get yourself together. Besides, those welfare clerks are mean as spit. When finally I got work and didn't need them anymore, I was making more money than they ever did. I guess meanness filled out their skimpy paychecks, which is why they treated us like beggars. More so when they looked at Lula Ann and back at me—like I was cheating or something. Things got better but I still had to be careful. Very careful in how I raised her. I had to be strict, very strict. Lula Ann needed to learn how to behave, how to keep her head down and not to make trouble. I don't care how many times she changes her name. Her color is a cross she will always carry. But it's not my fault. It's not my fault. It's not my fault. It's not.

Bride

I'm scared. Something bad is happening to me. I feel like I'm melting away. I can't explain it to you but I do know when it started. It began after he said, "You not the woman I want."

"Neither am I."

I still don't know why I said that. It just popped out of my mouth. But when he heard my sassy answer he shot me a hateful look before putting on his jeans. Then he grabbed his boots and T-shirt and when I heard the door slam I wondered for a split second if he was not just ending our silly argument, but ending us, our relationship. Couldn't be. Any minute I would hear the key turn, the front door click open and close. But I didn't hear anything the whole night. Nothing at all. What? I'm not exciting enough? Or pretty enough? I can't have thoughts of my own? Do things he doesn't approve of? By morning soon as I woke up I was furious. Glad he was gone because clearly he was just using me since I had money and a crotch. I was so angry, if you had seen me you would have thought I had spent those six months with him in a holding cell without arraignment or a lawyer, and suddenly the judge called the whole thing off—dismissed the case or refused to hear it at all. Anyway I refused to whine, wail or accuse. He said one thing; I agreed. Fuck him. Besides, our affair wasn't all that spectacular—not even the mildly dangerous sex I used to let myself enjoy. Well, anyway it was nothing like those double-page spreads in fashion magazines, you know, couples standing half naked in surf, looking so fierce and downright mean, their sexuality like lightning and the sky going dark to show off the shine of their skin. I love those ads. But our affair didn't even measure up to any old R-&-B song—some tune with a beat arranged to generate fever. It wasn't even the sugary lyrics of a thirties blues song: "Baby, baby, why you treat me so? I do anything you say, go anywhere you want me to go." Why I kept comparing us to magazine spreads and music I can't say, but it tickled me to settle on "I Wanna Dance with Somebody."

It was raining the next day. Bullet taps on the windows followed by crystal lines of water. I avoided the temptation to glance through the panes at the sidewalk beneath my condo. Besides, I knew what was out there—nasty-looking palm trees lining the road, benches in that tacky little park, few if any pedestrians, a sliver of sea far beyond. I fought giving in to any wish that he was coming back. When a tiny ripple of missing him surfaced, I beat it back. Around noon I opened a bottle of Pinot Grigio and sank into the sofa, its suede and silk cushions as comfy as any arms. Almost. Because I have to admit he is one beautiful man, flawless even, except for a tiny scar on his upper lip and an ugly one on his shoulder—an orange-red blob with a tail. Otherwise, head to toe, he is one gorgeous man. I'm not so bad myself, so imagine how we looked as a couple. After a glass or two of the wine I was a little buzzed, and decided to call my friend Brooklyn, tell her all about it. How he hit me harder than a fist with six words: You not the woman I want. How they rattled me so I agreed with them. So stupid. But then I changed my mind about calling her. You know how it is. Nothing new. Just he walked out and I don't know why. Besides, too much was happening at the office for me to bother my best friend and colleague with gossip about another breakup. Especially now. I'm regional manager now and that's like being a captain so I have to maintain the right relationship with the crew. Our company, Sylvia, Inc., is a small cosmetics business, but it's beginning to blossom and make waves, finally, and shed its frumpy past. It used to be Sylph Corsets for Discriminating Women back in the forties, but changed its name and ownership to Sylvia Apparel, then to Sylvia, Inc., before going flat-out hip with six cool cosmetics lines, one of which is mine. I named it YOU, GIRL: Cosmetics for Your Personal Millennium. It's for girls and women of all complexions from ebony to lemonade to milk. And it's mine, all mine—the idea, the brand, the campaign.

Wiggling my toes under the silk cushion I couldn't help smiling at the lipstick smile on my wineglass, thinking, "How about that, Lula Ann? Did you ever believe you would grow up to be this hot, or this successful?" Maybe *she* was the woman he wanted. But Lula Ann Bridewell is no longer available and she was never a woman. Lula Ann was a sixteen-year-old-me who dropped that dumb countryfied name as soon as I left high school. I was Ann Bride for two years until I interviewed for a sales job at Sylvia, Inc., and, on a hunch, shortened my name to Bride, with nothing anybody needs to say before or after that one memorable syllable. Customers and reps like it, but he ignored it. He called me "baby" most of the time. "Hey, baby"; "Come on, baby." And sometimes "You my girl," accent on the *my*. The only time he said "woman" was the day he split.

The more white wine the more I thought good riddance. No more dallying with a mystery man with no visible means of support. An ex-felon if ever there was one, though he laughed when I teased him about how he spent his time when I was at the office: Idle? Roaming? Or meeting someone? He said his Saturday afternoon trips downtown were not reports to a probation officer or drug rehab counselor. Yet he never told me what they were. I told him every single thing about myself; he confided nothing, so I just made stuff up with TV plots: he was an informant with a new identity, a disbarred lawyer. Whatever. I didn't really care.

Actually the timing of his leaving was perfect for me. With him gone out of my life and out of my apartment I could concentrate on the launch of YOU, GIRL and, equally important, keep a promise I'd made to myself long before I met him—we fought about it the night he said "You not the woman. . . ." According to prisoninfo.org/paroleboard/calendar, it was time. I'd been planning this trip for a year, choosing carefully what a parolee would need: I saved up five thousand dollars in cash over the years, and bought a three-thousand-dollar Continental Airlines gift certificate. I put a promotional box of YOU, GIRL into a brand-new Louis Vuitton shopping bag, all of which could take her anywhere. Comfort her, anyway; help her forget and take the edge off bad luck, hopelessness and boredom. Well, maybe not boredom, no prison is a convent. He didn't understand why I was so set on going and the night when we quarreled about my promise, he ran off. I guess I threatened his ego by doing some Good Samaritan thing not directed at him. Selfish bastard. I paid the rent, not him, and the maid too. When we went to clubs and concerts we rode in my beautiful Jaguar or in cars I hired. I bought him beautiful shirts—although he never wore them—and did all the shopping. Besides, a promise is a promise, especially if it's to oneself.

It was when I got dressed for the drive I noticed the first peculiar thing. Every bit of my pubic hair was gone. Not gone as in shaved or waxed, but gone as in erased, as in never having been there in the first place. It scared me, so I threaded through the hair on my head to see if it was shedding, but it was as thick and slippery as it had always been. Allergy? Skin disease, maybe? It worried me but there was no time to do more than be anxious and plan to see a dermatologist. I had to be on my way to make it on time.

I suppose other people might like the scenery bordering this highway but it's so thick with lanes, exits, parallel roads, overpasses, cautionary signals and signs it's like being forced to read a newspaper while driving. Annoying. Along with amber alerts, silver and gold ones were springing up. I stayed in the right lane and slowed down because from past drives out this way I knew the Norristown exit was easy to miss and the prison had no sign of its existence in the world for a mile beyond the exit ramp. I guess they didn't want tourists to know that some of the reclaimed desert California is famous for holds evil women. Decagon Women's Correctional Center, right outside Norristown, owned by a private company, is worshipped by the locals for the work it provides: serving visitors, guards, clerical staff, cafeteria workers, health care folks and most of all construction laborers repairing the road and fences and adding wing after wing to house the increasing flood of violent, sinful women committing bloody female crimes. Lucky for the state, crime does pay.

The couple of times I drove to Decagon before, I never tried to get inside on some pretext or other. Back then I just wanted to see where the lady monster—that's what they called her—had been caged for fifteen of her twenty-five-to-life sentence. This time was different. She has been granted parole and, according to penal review notices, Sofia Huxley is going to strut through the bars I pushed her behind.

You'd think with Decagon being all about corporate money that a Jaguar wouldn't stand out. But behind the curbside buses, old Toyotas and secondhand trucks, my car, sleek, rat gray with a vanity license, looked like a gun. But it was not as sinister as the white limousines I've seen parked there—engines snoring, chauffeurs leaning against gleaming fenders. Tell me, who would need a driver leaping to open the door and make a quick getaway? A grand madam impatient to get back to her designer linens in her tasteful high-rise brothel? Or maybe a teenage hookerette eager to get back to the patio of some sumptuous, degenerate private club where she could celebrate her release among friends by ripping up her prison-issue underwear. No Sylvia, Inc., products for her. Our line is sexy enough but not expensive enough. Like all sex trash, the little hookerette would think the higher the price, the better the quality. If she only knew. Still, she might buy some YOU, GIRL sparkle eye shadow or gold-flecked lip gloss.

No limousines today, unless you count the Lincoln town car. Mostly just worn Toyotas and ancient Chevys, silent grown-ups and jittery children. An old man sitting at the bus stop is digging into a box of Cheerios, trying to find the last circle of sweet oat bran. He's wearing ancient wing-tip shoes and crisp new jeans. His baseball cap, his brown vest over a white shirt, scream Salvation Army store but his manner is superior, dainty, even. His legs are crossed and he examines the bit of dry cereal as though it were a choice grape picked especially for him by groundskeepers to the throne.

Four o'clock; it won't be long now. Huxley, Sofia, a.k.a. 0071140, won't be released during visiting hours. At exactly four-thirty only the town car is left, owned probably by a lawyer with an alligator briefcase full of papers, money and cigarettes. The cigarettes for his client, the money for witnesses, the papers to look like he's working.

"Are you okay, Lula Ann?" The prosecutor's voice was soft, encouraging, but I could barely hear her. "There's nothing to be afraid of. She can't hurt you."

No, she can't and, damn, here she is. Number 0071140. Even after fifteen years I could never mistake her simply because of her height, six feet at least. Nothing has shrunk the giant I remember who was taller than the bailiff, the judge, the lawyers and almost as tall as the police. Only her co-monster husband matched her height. Nobody doubted she was the filthy freak that parents shaking with anger called her. "Look at her eyes," they whispered. Everywhere in the courthouse, ladies' room, on benches lining the halls they whispered: "Cold, like the snake she is." "At twenty? How could a twenty-year-old do those things to children?" "Are you kidding? Just look at those eyes. Old as dirt." "My little boy will never get over it." "Devil." "Bitch."

Now those eyes are more like a rabbit's than a snake's but the height is the same. A whole lot else has changed. She is as thin as a rope. Size 1 panties; an A-cup bra, if any. And she could sure use some GlamGlo. Formalize Wrinkle Softener and Juicy Bronze would give color to the whey color of her skin.

When I step out of the Jaguar I don't wonder or care whether she recognizes me. I just walk over to her and say, "Need a lift?"

She throws me a quick, uninterested glance and turns her gaze to the road. "No. I don't."

Her mouth is trembly. It used to be hard, a straight razor sharpened to slice a kid. A little Botox and some Tango-Matte, not glitter, would have softened her lips and maybe influenced the jury in her favor except there was no YOU, GIRL back then.

"Somebody picking you up?" I smile.

"Taxi," she says.

Funny. She is answering a stranger dutifully like she's

used to it. No "What's it to you?" or even "Who the hell are you?" but going on to explain further. "Called a cab. I mean the desk did."

When I come closer and reach out to touch her arm the cab rolls up and fast as a bullet she grabs the door handle, tosses in her little carrier bag and slams the door shut. I bang on the window shouting, "Wait! Wait!" Too late. The driver negotiates the U-turn like a NASCAR pro.

I rush to my car. Following them isn't hard. I even pass the taxi to disguise the fact that I am tailing her. That turns out to be a mistake. Just as I'm about to enter the exit ramp, I see the taxi shoot ahead of me toward Norristown. Gravel pings my wheels as I brake, reverse and follow them. The road to Norristown is lined with neat, uniform houses built in the fifties and added on repeatedly—a closed side porch, a garage expanded for two cars, backyard patio. The road looks like a kindergarten drawing of light-blue, white or yellow houses with pine-green or beet-red doors sitting smugly on wide lawns. All that is missing is a pancake sun with ray sticks all around it. Beyond the houses, next to a mall as pale and sad as "lite" beer, a sign announces the beginning of the town. Next to it another, bigger sign for Eva Dean's Motel and Restaurant. The taxi turns and stops by the entrance. She gets out and pays the driver. I follow and park a ways back near the restaurant. Only one other car is in the parking area—a black SUV. I am sure she is meeting someone, but after a few minutes at the check-in desk, she goes straight to the restaurant and takes a seat by the window. I can see her clearly and watch her study the menu like a remedial or English-as-a-second-language student—lip-reading, running her finger over the items. What a change. This is the teacher who had kindergartners cut apples into rings to shape the letter *O,* doled out pretzels as *B*'s, slit watermelon chunks into *Y*'s. All to spell BOY—who she liked best according to the women whispering in front of the sinks in the ladies' room. Fruit as bait was a big part of the trial's testimony.

Look at her eat. The waitress keeps placing plate after plate in front of her. Makes sense, sort of, this first out-of-prison meal. She's gobbling like a refugee, like somebody who's been floating at sea without food or water for weeks and just about to wonder what harm it would do to his dying boatmate to taste his flesh before it shrank. She never takes her eyes from the food, stabbing, slicing, scooping helter-skelter among the dishes. She drinks no water, butters no bread, as though nothing is allowed to delay her speed-eating. The whole thing is over in ten or twelve minutes. Then she pays, leaves and hurries down the walkway. Now what? Key in hand, tote bag on her shoulder, she stops and turns in to a break between two stucco walls. I get out of the car and walk-run behind her until I hear the retching sounds of vomit. So I hide behind the SUV until she comes out.

3-A is painted on the door she unlocks. I'm ready. I make sure my knock is authoritative, strong but not threatening.

"Yes?" Her voice is shaky, the humble sound of someone trained to automatic obedience.

"Mrs. Huxley. Open the door, please."

There is silence then, "I uh. I'm sorta sick."

"I know," I say. A trace of judgment in my voice, hoping she thinks it's about the sick she left on the pavement. "Open the door."

She opens it and stands there barefoot with a towel in her hand. She wipes her mouth. "Yes?"

"We need to talk."

"Talk?" She blinks rapidly but doesn't ask the real question: "Who are you?"

I push past her, leading with the Louis Vuitton bag. "You're Sofia Huxley, right?"

She nods. A tiny flash of fear is in her eyes. I'm black as midnight and dressed in all white so maybe she thinks it's a uniform and I'm an authority of some sort. I want to calm her so I hold up the shopping bag and say, "Come on. Let's sit down. I have something for you." She doesn't look at the bag or my face; she stares at my shoes with their high lethal heels and dangerously pointed toes.

"What do you want me to do?" she asks.

Such a soft, accommodating voice. Knowing after fifteen years behind bars that nothing is free. Nobody gives away anything at no cost to the receiver. Whatever it is—

cigarettes, magazines, tampons, stamps, Mars bars or a jar of peanut butter—it comes with strings tough as fishing line.

"Nothing. I don't want you to do a thing."

Now her eyes stray from my shoes to my face, opaque eyes without inquiry. So I answer the question a normal person would have posed. "I saw you leave Decagon. No one was there to meet you. I offered you a lift."

"That was you?" She frowns.

"Me. Yes."

"I know you?"

"My name is Bride."

She squints. "That supposed to mean something to me?"

"No," I say and smile. "Look what I brought you." I can't resist and place the bag on the bed. I reach inside and on top of the gift package of YOU, GIRL I lay two envelopes— the slim one with the airline gift certificate then the fat one with five thousand dollars. About two hundred dollars for each year if she had served her full sentence.

Sofia stares at the display as though the items might be infected. "What's all that for?"

I wonder if prison has done something to her brain. "It's okay," I say. "Just a few things to help you."

"Help me what?"

"Get a good start. You know, on your life."

"My life?" Something is wrong. She sounds as if she needs an introduction to the word.

"Yeah." I am still smiling. "Your new life."

"Why? Who sent you?" She looks interested now, not frightened.

"I guess you don't remember me." I shrug. "Why would you? Lula Ann. Lula Ann Bridewell. At the trial? I was one of the children who—"

I search through the blood with my tongue. My teeth are all there, but I can't seem to get up. I can feel my left eyelid shutting down and my right arm is dead. The door opens and all the gifts I brought are thrown at me, one by one, including the Vuitton bag. The door slams shut, then opens again. My black stiletto-heeled shoe lands on my back before rolling off next to my left arm. I reach for it and am relieved to learn that, unlike the right one, this one can move. I try to scream "help," but my mouth belongs to somebody else. I crawl a few feet and try to stand. My legs work, so I gather up the gifts, push them into the bag and, one shoe on, one left behind, limp to my car. I don't feel anything. I don't think anything. Not until I see my face in the side-view mirror. My mouth looks as though it's stuffed with raw liver; the whole side of my face is scraped of skin; my right eye is a mushroom. All I want to do is get away from here—no 911; it takes too long and I don't want some ignorant motel manager staring at me. Police. There have to be some in this town. Igniting, shifting, steering with a left hand, while the other one lies dead next to my thigh, takes concentration. All of it. So it's not until I get farther into

21

Norristown and see a sign with an arrow pointing to the police station that it hits me—the cops will write a report, interview the accused and take a picture of my wrecked face as evidence. And what if the local newspaper gets the story along with my photograph? Embarrassment would be nothing next to the jokes directed at YOU, GIRL. From YOU, GIRL to BOO, GIRL.

Hammers of pain make it hard to get out my cellphone and dial Brooklyn, the one person I can trust. Completely.

Brooklyn

She's lying. We are sitting in this dump of a clinic after I've driven over two hours to find this hick town, then I have to locate her car parked in the rear of a closed-shut police station. Of course it's closed; it's Sunday, when only churches and Wal-Mart are open. She was hysterical when I found her bloody and crying out of one eye, the other one too swollen to shed water. Poor thing. Somebody ruined one of those eyes, the ones that spooked everybody with their strangeness—large, slanted, slightly hooded and funny-colored, considering how black her skin is. Alien eyes, I call them, but guys think they're gorgeous, of course.

Well, when I find this little emergency clinic facing the mall's parking lot I have to hold her up to help her walk. She hobbles, wearing one shoe. Finally we get a nurse's bug-eyed attention. She is startled at the pair of us: one white girl with blond dreads, one very black one with silky curls. It takes forever to sign stuff and show insurance cards. Then we sit down to wait for the on-call doctor who lives, I don't know, far off in some other crappy town. Bride doesn't say a word while I drive her here, but in the waiting room she starts the lie.

"I'm ruined," she whispers.

I say, "No you're not. Give it time. Remember what Grace looked like after her face tuck?"

"A surgeon did her face," she answers. "A maniac did mine."

I press her. "So tell me. What happened, Bride? Who was he?"

"Who was who?" She touches her nose tenderly while breathing through her mouth.

"The guy who beat you half to death."

She coughs for some time and I hand her a tissue. "Did I say it was a guy? I don't remember saying it was a guy."

"Are you telling me a woman did this?"

"No," she says. "No. It was a guy."

"Was he trying to rape you?"

"I suppose. Somebody scared him off, I guess. He banged me around and took off."

See what I mean? Not even a good lie. I push a bit more. "He didn't take your purse, wallet, anything?"

She mumbles, "Boy Scout, I guess." Her lips are puffy and her tongue can't manage consonants but she tries to smile at her own stupid joke.

"Why didn't whoever scared him off stay and help you?"

"I don't know! I don't know! I don't know!"

She is shouting and fake-sobbing so I back off. Her single open eye isn't up to it and her mouth must hurt too much to keep it up. For five minutes I don't say a word, just flip through the pages of a *Reader's Digest;* then I try to make my voice sound as normal and conversational as I can. I decide not to ask why she called me instead of her lover man.

"What were you doing up here anyway?"

"I came to see a friend." She bends forward as though her stomach hurts.

"In Norristown? Your friend lives here?"

"No. Nearby."

"You find him?"

"Her. No. I never found her."

"Who is she?"

"Somebody from a long time ago. She wasn't there. Probably dead by now."

She knows I know she's lying. Why wouldn't an attacker take her money? Something has rattled her brainpan otherwise why would she tell me such fucked-up lies? I guess she doesn't give a damn what I think. When I stuffed her little white skirt and top into the shopping bag, I found a rubber band around fifty hundred-dollar bills, an airline gift certificate and samples of YOU, GIRL not yet launched. Okay? No species of would-be rapist would want Nude Skin Glo, but free cash? I decide to let it go and wait until she's seen the doctor.

Afterward, when Bride holds up my compact mirror to

her face, I know what she sees will break her heart. A quarter of her face is fine; the rest is cratered. Ugly black stitches, puffy eye, bandages on her forehead, lips so Ubangi she can't pronounce the *r* in *raw,* which is what her skin looks like—all pink and blue-black. Worse than anything is her nose—nostrils wide as an orangutan's under gauze the size of half a bagel. Her beautiful unbruised eye seems to cower, bloodshot, practically dead.

I shouldn't be thinking this. But her position at Sylvia, Inc., might be up for grabs. How can she persuade women to improve their looks with products that can't improve her own? There isn't enough YOU, GIRL foundation in the world to hide eye scars, a broken nose and facial skin scraped down to pink hypodermis. Assuming much of the damage fades, she will still need plastic surgery, which means weeks and weeks of idleness, hiding behind glasses and floppy hats. I might be asked to take over. Temporarily, of course.

"I can't eat. I can't talk. I can't think."

Her voice is whiny and she is trembling.

I put my arm around her and whisper, "Hey, girlfriend, no pity party. Let's get out of this dump. They don't even have private rooms and that nurse had lettuce in her teeth and I doubt she's washed her hands since graduating from that online nursing course she took."

Bride stops shaking, adjusts the sling holding her right

arm and asks me, "You don't think that doctor did a good job?"

"Who knows?" I say. "In this trailer park clinic? I'm driving you to a real hospital—with a toilet and sink in the room."

"Don't they have to release me?" She sounds like a ten-year-old.

"Please. We're leaving. Now. Look what I bought while you were being patched up. Sweats and flip-flops. No decent hospital in these parts but a very respectable Wal-Mart. Come on. Up. Lean on me. Where did Florence Nightingale put your things? We'll get some ice pops or slurries on the way. Or a milk shake. That's probably better medicine-wise—or some tomato juice, chicken broth, maybe."

I'm rambling, fussing with pills and clothes while she clutches that ugly flowered hospital gown. "Oh, Bride," I say, but my voice cracks. "Don't look like that—it's going to be all right."

I have to drive slowly; every bump or sudden lane switch makes her wince or grunt. I try to get her mind off her pain.

"I didn't know you were twenty-three. I thought you were my age, twenty-one. I saw it on your driver's license. You know, when I was looking for your insurance card."

She doesn't answer, so I keep on trying to get a smile out of her. "But your good eye looks twenty."

It doesn't work. What the hell. I might as well be talking to myself. I decide to just get her home and settled. I'll take care of everything at work. Bride will be on sick leave for a long time, and somebody has to take on her responsibilities. And who knows how that might turn out?

Bride

She really was a freak. Sofia Huxley. The quick change from obedient ex-con to raging alligator. From slack-lipped to fangs. From slouch to hammer. I never saw the signal—no eye squint or grip of neck cords, no shoulder flex or raised lip showing teeth. Nothing announced her attack on me. I'll never forget it, and even if I tried to, the scars, let alone the shame, wouldn't let me.

Memory is the worst thing about healing. I lie around all day with nothing urgent to do. Brooklyn has taken care of explanations to the office staff: attempted rape, foiled, blah, blah. She is a true friend and doesn't annoy me like those fake ones who come here just to gaze and pity me. I can't watch television; it's so boring—mostly blood, lipstick, and the haunches of anchorgirls. What passes for news is either gossip or a lecture of lies. How can I take crime shows seriously where the female detectives track killers in Louboutin heels? As for reading, print makes me dizzy, and for some reason I don't like listening to music anymore. Vocals, both the beautiful and the mediocre, depress me, and instrumentals are worse. Plus something bad has been done to my tongue because my taste buds have disappeared. Everything tastes like lemons—except lemons, which taste like salt. Wine is a waste since Vicodin gives me a thicker, more comfortable fog.

The bitch didn't even hear me out. I wasn't the only witness, the only one who turned Sofia Huxley into 0071140. There was lots of other testimony about her molestations. At least four other kids were witnesses. I didn't hear what they said but they were shaking and crying when they left the courtroom. The social worker and psychologist who coached us put their arms around them, whispering, "You'll be fine. You did great." Neither one hugged me but they smiled at me. Apparently Sofia Huxley has no family. Well she has a husband who is in another prison and still unparoled after seven tries. No one was there to meet her. Nobody. So why didn't she just accept help instead of whatever check-out-counter or cleaning-woman job she might be given? Rich parolees don't end up cleaning toilets at Wendy's.

I was only eight years old, still little Lula Ann, when I lifted my arm and pointed my finger at her.

"Is the woman you saw here in this room?" The lawyer lady smells of tobacco.

I nod.

"You have to speak, Lula. Say 'yes' or 'no.'"

"Yes."

"Can you show us where she is seated?"

I am afraid of knocking over the paper cup of water the lady lawyer gave me.

"Relax," says the prosecutor lady. "Take your time."

And I did take my time. My hand was in a fist until my arm was straight. Then I unfolded my forefinger. *Pow!* Like a cap pistol. Mrs. Huxley stared at me then opened her mouth as though about to say something. She looked shocked, unbelieving. But my finger still pointed, pointed so long the lady prosecutor had to touch my hand and say, "Thank you, Lula," to get me to put my arm down. I glanced at Sweetness; she was smiling like I've never seen her smile before—with mouth and eyes. And that wasn't all. Outside the courtroom all the mothers smiled at me, and two actually touched and hugged me. Fathers gave me thumbs-up. Best of all was Sweetness. As we walked down the court-house steps she held my hand, my hand. She never did that before and it surprised me as much as it pleased me because I always knew she didn't like touching me. I could tell. Distaste was all over her face when I was little and she had to bathe me. Rinse me, actually, after a halfhearted rub with a soapy washcloth. I used to pray she would slap my face or spank me just to feel her touch. I made little mistakes deliberately, but she had ways to punish me without touching the skin she hated—bed without supper, lock me in my room—but her screaming at me was the worst. When fear rules, obedience is the only survival choice. And I was good at it. I behaved and behaved and behaved. Frightened as I was to appear in court, I did what the teacher-psychologists expected of me. Brilliantly, I know, because after the trial Sweetness was kind of motherlike.

I don't know. Maybe I'm just mad more at myself than at Mrs. Huxley. I reverted to the Lula Ann who never fought back. Ever. I just lay there while she beat the shit out of me. I could have died on the floor of that motel room if her face hadn't gone apple-red with fatigue. I didn't make a sound, didn't even raise a hand to protect myself when she slapped my face then punched me in the ribs before smashing my jaw with her fist then butting my head with hers. She was panting when she dragged and threw me out the door. I can still feel her hard fingers clenching the hair at the back of my neck, her foot on my behind and I can still hear the crack of my bones hitting concrete. Elbow, jaw. I feel my arms sliding and grabbing for balance. Then my tongue searching through blood to locate my teeth. When the door slammed then opened again so she could throw out my shoe, like a whipped puppy I just crawled away afraid to even whimper.

Maybe he is right. I am not the woman. When he left I shook it off and pretended it didn't matter.

Foam spurting from an aerosol can made him chuckle, so he lathered with shaving soap and a brush, a handsome thing of boar's hair swelling from an ivory handle. I think it's in the trash along with his toothbrush, strop and straight razor. The things he left are too alive. It's time to throw all of it out. He left everything: toiletries, clothes and a cloth bag containing two books, one in a foreign language, the other a book of poems. I dump it all, then pick through the trash and take out his shaving brush and bone-handled razor. I put them both in the medicine cabinet and when I close the door I stare at my face in the mirror.

"You should always wear white, Bride. Only white and all white all the time." Jeri, calling himself a "total person" designer, insisted. Looking for a makeover for my second interview at Sylvia, Inc., I consulted him.

"Not only because of your name," he told me, "but because of what it does to your licorice skin," he said. "And black is the new black. Know what I mean? Wait. You're more Hershey's syrup than licorice. Makes people think of whipped cream and chocolate soufflé every time they see you."

That made me laugh. "Or Oreos?"

"Never. Something classy. Bonbons. Hand-dipped."

At first it was boring shopping for white-only clothes until I learned how many shades of white there were: ivory, oyster, alabaster, paper white, snow, cream, ecru, Champagne, ghost, bone. Shopping got even more interesting when I began choosing colors for accessories.

Jeri, advising me, said, "Listen, Bride baby. If you must have a drop of color limit it to shoes and purses, but I'd keep both black when white simply won't do. And don't forget: no makeup. Not even lipstick or eyeliner. None."

I asked him about jewelry. Gold? Some diamonds? An emerald brooch?

"No. No." He threw his hands up. "No jewelry at all. Pearl dot earrings, maybe. No. Not even that. Just you, girl. All sable and ice. A panther in snow. And with your body? And those wolverine eyes? Please!"

I took his advice and it worked. Everywhere I went I got double takes but not like the faintly disgusted ones I used to get as a kid. These were adoring looks, stunned but hungry. Plus, unbeknownst to him, Jeri had given me the name for a product line. YOU, GIRL.

My face looks almost new in the mirror. My lips are back to normal; so are my nose and my eye. Only my rib area is still tender and, to my surprise, the scraped skin on my face has healed the quickest. I look almost beautiful again, so why am I still sad? On impulse I open the medicine cabinet and take out his shaving brush. I finger it. The silky hair is both tickly and soothing. I bring the brush to my chin, stroke it the way he used to. I move it to the underside of my jaw, then up to my earlobes. For some reason I feel faint. Soap. I need lather. I tear open a fancy box containing a tube of body foam "for the skin he loves." Then I squeeze it into the soap dish and wet his brush. Slathering the foam on my face I am breathless. I lather my cheeks, under my nose. This is crazy I'm sure but I stare at my face. My eyes look wider and starry. My nose is not only healed, it's perfect, and my lips between the white foam look so downright kissable I touch them with the tip of my little finger. I don't want to stop, but I have to. I clasp his razor. How did he hold it? Some finger arrangement I don't remember. I'll have to practice. Meantime I use the dull edge and carve dark chocolate lanes through swirls of white lather. I splash water and rinse my face. The satisfaction that follows is so so sweet.

This working from home isn't as bad as I thought it would be. I have authority still, although Brooklyn second-guesses me, even overrides a few of my decisions. I don't mind. I'm lucky she has my back. Besides, when I feel depressed the cure is tucked away in a little kit where his shaving equipment is. Lathering warm soapy water, I can hardly wait for the brushing and then the razor, the combination that both excites and soothes me. Lets me imagine without grief times when I was made fun of and hurt.

"She's sort of pretty under all that black." Neighbors and their daughters agreed. Sweetness never attended parent-teacher meetings or volleyball games. I was encouraged to take business courses not the college track, community college instead of four-year state universities. I didn't do any of that. After I don't know how many refusals, I finally got a job working stock—never sales where customers would see me. I wanted the cosmetics counter but didn't dare ask for it. I got to be a buyer only after rock-dumb white girls got promotions or screwed up so bad they settled for somebody who actually knew about stock. Even the interview at Sylvia, Inc., got off to a bad start. They questioned my style, my clothes and told me to come back later. That's when I consulted Jeri. Then walking down the hall toward the interviewer's office, I could see the effect I was having: wide admiring eyes, grins and whispers: "Whoa!" "Oh, baby." In no time I rocketed to regional manager. "See?" said Jeri. "Black sells. It's the hottest commodity in the civilized world. White girls, even brown girls have to strip naked to get that kind of attention."

True or not, it made me, remade me. I began to move differently—not a strut, not that pelvis-out rush of the runway—but a stride, slow and focused. Men leaped and I let myself be caught. For a while, anyway, until my sex life became sort of like Diet Coke—deceptively sweet minus nutrition. More like a PlayStation game imitating the safe glee of virtual violence and just as brief. All my boyfriends were typecast: would-be actors, rappers, professional athletes, players waiting for my crotch or my paycheck like an allowance; others, already having made it, treating me like a medal, a shiny quiet testimony to their prowess. Not one of them giving, helpful—none interested in what I thought, just what I looked like. Joking or baby-talking me through what I believed was serious conversation before they found more ego props elsewhere. I remember one date in particular, a medical student who persuaded me to join him on a visit to his parents' house up north. As soon as he introduced me it was clear I was there to terrorize his family, a means of threat to this nice old white couple.

"Isn't she beautiful?" he kept repeating. "Look at her, Mother? Dad?" His eyes were gleaming with malice.

But they outclassed him with their warmth—however faked—and charm. His disappointment was obvious, his anger thinly repressed. His parents even drove me to the train stop, probably so I wouldn't have to put up with his failed racist joke on them. I was relieved, even knowing what the mother did with my used teacup.

Such was the landscape of men.

Then him. Booker. Booker Starbern.

I don't want to think about him now. Or how empty, how trivial and lifeless everything seems now. I don't want to remember how handsome he is, perfect except for that ugly burn scar on his shoulder. I stroked every inch of his golden skin, sucked his earlobes. I know the quality of the hair in his armpit; I fingered the dimple in his upper lip; I poured red wine in his navel and drank its spill. There is no place on my body his lips did not turn into bolts of lightning. Oh, God. I have to stop reliving our lovemaking. I have to forget how new it felt every single time, both fresh and somehow eternal. I'm tone-deaf but fucking him made me sing and then, and then out of nowhere, "You not the woman . . ." before vanishing like a ghost.

Dismissed.

Erased.

Even Sofia Huxley, of all people, erased me. A convict. A convict! She could have said, "No thanks," or even "Get out!" No. She went postal. Maybe fistfighting is prison talk. Instead of words, broken bones and drawing blood is inmate conversation. I'm not sure which is worse, being dumped like trash or whipped like a slave.

We had lunch in my office the day before he split— lobster salad, Smartwater, peach slices in brandy. Oh, stop. I can't keep thinking about him. And I'm stir-crazy slouching around these rooms. Too much light, too much space, too lonely. I have to put on some clothes and get out of here. Do what Brooklyn keeps nagging me about: forget sunglasses and floppy hats, show myself, live life like it really is life. She should know; she's making Sylvia, Inc., her own.

I choose carefully: bone-white shorts and halter, high-wedged rope-and-straw sandals, beige canvas tote into which I drop the shaving brush in case I need it. *Elle* magazine and sunglasses too. Brooklyn would approve even though I'm just going two blocks to a park used mostly by dog walkers and seniors this time of day. Later on there will be joggers and skaters, but no mothers and children on a Saturday. Their weekends are for playdates, playrooms, playgrounds and play restaurants, all guarded by loving nannies with delicious accents.

I select a bench near an artificial pond where real ducks sail. And though I quickly block a memory of his describing the difference between wild drakes and yardbirds, my muscles remember his cool, massaging fingers. While I turn the pages of *Elle* and scan pictures of the young and eatable, I hear slow steps on gravel. I look up. The steps belong to a gray-haired couple strolling by, silent, holding hands. Their paunches are the exact same size, although his is lower down. Both wear colorless slacks and loose T-shirts imprinted with faded signs, front and back, about peace. The teenage dog walkers snigger and yank leashes for no reason, except perhaps envy of a long life of intimacy. The couple moves carefully, as though in a dream. Steps matching, looking straight ahead like people called to a spaceship where a door will slide open and a tongue of red carpet rolls out. They will ascend, hand in hand, into the arms of a benevolent Presence. They will hear music so beautiful it will bring you to tears.

That does it. The hand-holding couple, their silent music. I can't stop it now—I'm back in the packed stadium. The screaming audience is no match for the wild, sexy music. Crowds dance in the aisles; people stand on their bench seats and clap to the drums. My arms are in the air waving to the music. My hips and head sway on their own. Before I see his face, his arms are around my waist, my back to his chest, his chin in my hair. Then his hands are on my stomach and I am dropping mine to hold on to his while we dance back to front. When the music stops I turn around to look at him. He smiles. I am moist and shivering.

Before I leave the park, I finger the bristles of the shaving brush. They are soft and warm.

Sweetness

Oh, yeah, I feel bad sometimes about how I treated Lula Ann when she was little. But you have to understand: I had to protect her. She didn't know the world. There was no point in being tough or sassy even when you were right. Not in a world where you could be sent to a juvenile lockup for talking back or fighting in school, a world where you'd be the last one hired and the first one fired. She couldn't know any of that or how her black skin would scare white people or make them laugh and trick her. I once saw a girl nowhere near as dark as Lula Ann and who couldn't be more than ten years old tripped by one of a group of white boys and when she fell and tried to scramble up another one put his foot on her behind and knocked her flat again. Those boys held their stomachs and bent over with laughter. Long after she got away, they were still giggling, so proud of themselves. If I hadn't been watching through the bus window I would have helped her, pulled her away from that white trash. See if I hadn't trained Lula Ann properly she wouldn't have known to always cross the street and avoid white boys. But the lessons I taught her paid off because in the end she made me proud as a peacock. It was in that case with that gang of pervert teachers—three of them, a man and two women—that she knocked it out of the park. Young as she was, she behaved like a grown-up on the witness stand—so calm and sure of herself. Fixing her wild hair was always a trial, but I braided it down tight for the court appearance and bought her a blue and white sailor dress. I was nervous thinking she would stumble getting up to the stand, or stutter, or forget what the psychologists said and put me to shame. But no, thank God, she put the noose, so to speak, around at least one of those sinful teachers' neck. The things they were accused of would make you puke. How they got little kids to do nasty things. It was in the newspapers and on television. For weeks, crowds of people with and without children in the school yelled outside the courthouse. Some had homemade signs saying, KILL THE FREAKS and NO MERCY FOR DEVILS.

I sat through most of the days of the trial, not all, just the days when Lula Ann was scheduled to appear, because many witnesses were postponed or never showed. They got sick or changed their minds. She looked scared but she stayed quiet, not like the other child witnesses fidgeting and whining. Some were even crying. After Lula Ann's performance in that court and on the stand I was so proud of her, we walked the streets hand in hand. It's not often you see a little black girl take down some evil whites. I wanted her to know how pleased I was so I had her ears pierced and bought her a pair of earrings—tiny gold hoops. Even the landlord smiled when he saw us. No pictures were in the newspapers because of privacy laws for children, but the word got out. The drugstore owner, who always turned his mouth down when he saw us together, handed Lula Ann a Clark bar after he heard about her courage.

I wasn't a bad mother, you have to know that, but I may have done some hurtful things to my only child because I had to protect her. Had to. All because of skin privileges. At first I couldn't see past all that black to know who she was and just plain love her. But I do. I really do. I think she understands now. I think so.

Last two times I saw her she was, well, striking. Kind of bold and confident. Each time she came I forgot just how black she really was because she was using it to her advantage in beautiful white clothes.

Taught me a lesson I should have known all along. What you do to children matters. And they might never forget. She's got a big-time job in California but she don't call or visit anymore. She sends me money and stuff every now and then, but I ain't seen her in I don't know how long.

Bride

Brooklyn picks the restaurant. Pirate, it's called, a semi-chic, once-hot, now barely-hanging-on place for tourists and the decidedly uncool. The evening is too chilly for the sleeveless white shift I'm wearing, but I want to impress Brooklyn with my progress, my barely visible scars. She is dragging me out of what she says is classic post-rape depression. Her cure is this overdesigned watering hole where male waiters in red suspenders emphasizing their bare chests will do the trick. She is a good friend. No pressure, she says. Just a quiet dinner in a mostly empty restaurant with cute but harmless beef on display. I know why she likes this place; she loves showing off around men. Long ago, before I met her, she twisted her blond hair into dreadlocks and, pretty as she is, the locks add an allure she wouldn't otherwise have. At least the black guys she dates think so.

We talk office gossip through the appetizer but the giggling stops when the mahimahi arrives. It's the usual over-the-top recipe, swimming in coconut milk, smothered with ginger, sesame seeds, garlic and teeny flakes of green onion. Annoyed by the chef's efforts to make a bland fish thrilling,

I scrape everything from the fillet and blurt out, "I want a vacation, to go somewhere. On a cruise ship."

Brooklyn grins. "Oooh. Where? Finally, some good news."

"But no kids," I say.

"That's easy. Fiji, maybe?"

"And no parties. I want to be with settled people with paunches. And play shuffleboard on a deck. Bingo too."

"Bride, you're scaring me." She dabs the napkin to a corner of her mouth and widens her eyes.

I put down my fork. "No, really. Just quiet. Nothing louder than waves lapping or ice melting in crystal glasses."

Brooklyn puts her elbow on the table and covers my hand with hers. "Aw, girl, you're still in shock. I'm not going to let you make any plans until this rape stuff wears off. You won't know what you want until then. Trust me, all right?"

I'm so tired of this. Next she'll be insisting I see a rape therapist or attend victim fests. I'm really sick of it because I need to be able to have an honest conversation with my closest friend. I bite the tip of an asparagus stalk then slowly cross my knife and fork.

"Look, I lied to you." I push my plate away so hard it knocks over what's left of my apple martini. I mop it up with my napkin carefully, trying to steady myself and make what I'm about to say sound normal. "I lied, girlfriend. I lied to you. Nobody tried to rape me and that was a woman beat the shit out of me. Somebody I was trying to help, for Christ's sake. I tried to help her and she would have killed me if she could."

Brooklyn stares open-mouthed then squints. "A woman? What woman? Who?"

"You don't know her."

"You don't either, obviously."

"I did once."

"Bride, don't give me scraps. Let me have the full plate, please." She pulls her locks behind her ears and fixes me with an intense glare.

It took maybe three minutes to tell it. How when I was a little girl in the second grade, a teacher in the kindergarten building next to the main building played dirty with her students.

"I can't hear this," says Brooklyn. She closes her eyes like a nun faced with porn.

"You asked for the full plate," I say.

"Okay, okay."

"Well, she was caught, tried, and sent away."

"Got it. So what's the problem?"

"I testified against her."

"Even better. So?"

"I pointed. I sat in the witness chair and pointed her out. Said I saw her do it."

"And?"

"They put her in prison. Gave her a twenty-five-year sentence."

"Good. End of story, no?"

"Well, no, not really." I am fidgeting, adjusting my neckline as well as my face. "I thought about her on and off, you know?"

"Uh, uh. Tell me."

"Well, she was just twenty."

"So were the Manson girls."

"In a few years she'll be forty and I thought she probably has no friends."

"Poor thing. No kiddies to rape in the joint. What a drag."

"You're not hearing me."

"Damn straight I'm not listening to you." Brooklyn slaps the table. "You nuts? Who is this female alligator, besides being pond scum, I mean. Is she related to you? What?"

"No."

"Well?"

"I just thought she would be sad, lonely after all these years."

"She's breathing. That not good enough for her?"

This is going nowhere. How can I expect her to understand? I signal the waiter. "Again," I say and nod toward my empty glass.

The waiter lifts his eyebrows and looks at Brooklyn. "None for me, cookie. I need cold sobriety."

He gives her a killer smile full of bright and bonded teeth.

"Look, Brooklyn, I don't know why I went. What I do know is I kept thinking about her. All these years in Decagon."

"You write to her? Visit?"

"No. I've seen her only twice. Once at the trial and then when this happened." I point to my face.

"You dumb bitch!" She seems really disgusted with me. "You put her behind bars! Of course she wants to mess you up."

"She wasn't like that before. She was gentle, funny, even, and kind."

"Before? Before what? You said you saw her twice—at the trial and when she clocked you. But what about seeing her diddling kids? You said—"

The waiter leans in with my drink.

"Okay." I'm irritable and it shows. "Three times."

Brooklyn tongues the corner of her mouth. "Say, Bride, did she molest you too? You can tell me."

Jesus. What does she think? That I'm a secret lesbian? In a company practically run by bi's, straights, trannies, gays and anybody who took their looks seriously. What's the point of closets these days?

"Oh, girl, don't be stupid." I shoot her the look Sweetness always put on when I spilled the Kool-Aid or tripped on the rug.

"Okay, okay." She waves her hand. "Waiter, honey, I've changed my mind. Belvedere. Rocks. Double it."

The waiter winks. "You got it," he says, hitting "got" with a slur that must have earned him a promising phone number in South Dakota.

"Look at me, girlfriend. Think about it. What made you feel so sorry for her? I mean, really."

"I don't know." I shake my head. "I guess I wanted to feel good about myself. Not so disposable. Sofia Huxley—that's her name—was all I could think of, someone who would appreciate some . . . something friendly without strings."

"Now I get it." She looks relieved and smiles at me.

"Do you? Really?"

"Absolutely. The dude splits, you feel like cow flop, you try to get your mojo back, but it's a bust, right?"

"Right. Sorta. I guess."

"So we fix it."

"How?" If anybody knows what to do, it's Brooklyn. Hitting the floor, she always says, requires a choice—lie there or bounce. "How do we fix it?"

"Well, not with no bingo." She's excited.

"What then?"

"Blingo!" she shouts.

"You called?" asks the waiter.

Two weeks later, just as she promised, Brooklyn organizes a celebration—a prelaunch party where I am the main attraction, the one who invented YOU, GIRL and helped create all the excitement about the brand. The location is a fancy hotel, I think. No, a smarty-pants museum. A crowd is waiting and so is a limousine. My hair, and dress are perfect: diamondlike jewels spangle the white lace of my gown, which is tight-fitting above the mermaidlike flounce at my ankles. It's transparent in interesting places but veiled in others—nipples and the naked triangle way below my navel.

All that's left is to choose earrings. I've lost my pearl dots, so I choose one-carat diamonds. Modest, nothing flashy, nothing to detract from what Jeri calls my black-coffee-and-whipped-cream palette. A panther in snow.

Christ. Now what? My earrings. They won't go in. The platinum stem keeps slipping away from my earlobe. I examine the earrings—nothing wrong. I peer at my lobes closely and discover the tiny holes are gone. Ridiculous. I've had pierced ears since I was eight years old. Sweetness gave me little circles of fake gold as a present after I testified against the Monster. Since then I've never worn clip-ons. Never. Pearl dots, usually, ignoring my "total person" designer, and sometimes, like now, diamonds. Wait. This is impossible. After all these years, I've got virgin earlobes, untouched by a needle, smooth as a baby's thumb? Maybe it's from the plastic surgery or side effects of the antibiotics? But that was weeks ago. I am trembling. I need the shaving brush. The phone is ringing. I get the brush out and stroke it lightly at my cleavage. It makes me dizzy. The phone keeps ringing. Okay, no jewelry, no earrings. I pick up the phone.

"Miss Bride, your driver is here."

If I pretend sleep maybe he will just get the hell out. Whoever he is I can't face him to chat or fake after-sex cuddle, especially since I don't remember any of it. He kisses my shoulder lightly, then fingers my hair. I murmur as though dreaming. I smile but keep my eyes closed. He moves the bedclothes and goes into the bathroom. I sneak a touch to my earlobes. Smooth. Still smooth. I am complimented constantly at the party—how beautiful, how pretty, so hot, so lovely, everyone says, but no one questions the absence of earrings. I find that strange, because all through the speeches, the award presentation, the dinner, the dancing, my baby thumb earlobes are so much on my mind I can't concentrate. So I deliver an incoherent thank-you speech, laugh too long at filthy jokes, stumble through conversations with coworkers, drink three, four times more than what I can gracefully hold. Do a single line, after which I flirt like a high school brat campaigning for prom queen, which is how I let whoever he is in my bed. I taste my tongue hoping the film is mine alone. God. Thank you. No handcuffs dangle from the bedposts.

He has finished showering and calls my name while putting his tuxedo back on. I don't answer; I don't look; I just pull the pillow over my head. That amuses him and I hear him chuckle. I listen to kitchen noises as he makes coffee. No, not coffee; I would smell it. He is pouring something—orange juice, V8, flat Champagne? That's all that's in the refrigerator. Silence, then footsteps. Please, please just leave. I hear a tick on the nightstand followed by the sound of my front door opening then closing. When I peep from under the pillow I see a folded square of paper next to the clock. Telephone number. FABULOUS. Then his name. I slump with relief. He is not an employee.

I rush to the bathroom and look in the wastebasket. Thank you, Jesus. A used condom. Traces of steam are on the shower glass near the medicine cabinet whose mirror is clear, sparkling, showing me what I saw last night—earlobes as chaste as the day I was born. So this is what insanity is. Not goofy behavior, but watching a sudden change in the world you used to know. I need the shaving brush, the soap. There is not a single hair in my armpit, but I lather it anyway. Now the other one. The lathering up, the shaving, calms me and I am so grateful I begin to think of other places that might need this little delight. My pudenda, perhaps. It's already hairless. Will it be too tricky using the straight razor down there? Tricky. Yes.

Calmed, I go back to bed and slide under the sheet. Minutes later my head explodes with throbbing pain. I get up and find two Vicodins to swallow. Waiting for the pills to work there is nothing to do but let my thoughts trail, track and bite one another.

What is happening to me?

My life is falling down. I'm sleeping with men whose names I don't know and not remembering any of it. What's going on? I'm young; I'm successful and pretty. Really pretty, so there! Sweetness. So why am I so miserable? Because he left me? I have what I've worked for and am good at it. I'm proud of myself, I really am, but it's the Vicodin and the hangover that make me keep remembering some not-so-proud junk in the past. I've gotten over all that and moved on. Even Booker thought so, didn't he? I spilled my guts to him, told him everything: every fear, every hurt, every accomplishment, however small. While talking to him certain things I had buried came up fresh as though I was seeing them for the first time—how Sweetness's bedroom always seemed unlit. I open the window next to her dresser. Her grown-up-woman stuff crowds her vanity: tweezers, cotton balls, that round box of Lucky Lady face powder, the blue bottle of Midnight in Paris cologne, hairpins in a tiny saucer, tissue, eyebrow pencils,

Maybelline mascara, Tabu lipstick. It's deep red and I try some on. No wonder I'm in the cosmetics business. It must have been describing all that stuff on Sweetness's dresser that made me tell him about that other thing. All about it. Me hearing a cat's meow through the open window, how pained it sounded, frightened, even. I looked. Down below in the walled area that led to the building's basement I saw not a cat but a man. He was leaning over the short, fat legs of a child between his hairy white thighs. The boy's little hands were fists, opening and closing. His crying was soft, squeaky and loaded with pain. The man's trousers were down around his ankles. I leaned over the windowsill and stared. The man had the same red hair as Mr. Leigh, the landlord, but I knew it couldn't be him because he was stern but not dirty. He demanded the rent be paid in cash before noon on the first day of the month and charged a late fee if you knocked on his door five minutes late. Sweetness was so scared of him she made sure I delivered the money first thing in the morning. I know now what I didn't know then—that standing up to Mr. Leigh meant having to look for another apartment. And that it would be hard finding a location in another safe, meaning mixed, neighborhood. So when I told Sweetness what I'd seen, she was furious. Not about a little crying boy, but about spreading the story. She wasn't interested in tiny fists or big hairy thighs; she was interested in keeping our apartment. She said, "Don't you say a word about it. Not to anybody, you hear me, Lula?

Forget it. Not a single word." So I was afraid to tell her the rest—that although I didn't make a sound, I just hung over the windowsill and stared, something made the man look up. And it was Mr. Leigh. He was zipping his pants while the boy lay whimpering between his boots. The look on his face scared me but I couldn't move. That's when I heard him shout, "Hey, little nigger cunt! Close that window and get the fuck outta there!"

When I told Booker about it I laughed at first, pretending the whole thing was just silly. Then I felt my eyes burning. Even before the tears welled, he held my head in the crook of his arm and pressed his chin in my hair.

"You never told anybody?" he asked me.

"Never," I said. "Only you."

"Now five people know. The boy, the freak, your mother, you and now me. Five is better than two but it should be five thousand."

He turned my face up to his and kissed me. "Did you ever see that boy again?"

I said I didn't think so, that he was down on the ground and I couldn't see his face. "All I know is that he was a white kid with brown hair." Then thinking of how his little fingers spread then curled, spread wide then curled tight I couldn't help sobbing.

"Come on, baby, you're not responsible for other folks' evil."

"I know, but—"

"No buts. Correct what you can; learn from what you can't."

"I don't always know what to correct."

"Yes you do. Think. No matter how hard we try to ignore it, the mind always knows truth and wants clarity."

That was one of the best talks we ever had. I felt such relief. No. More than that. I felt curried, safe, owned.

Not like now, twisting and turning between the most expensive cotton sheets in the world. Aching, waiting for another Vicodin to start up while fretting in my gorgeous bedroom, unable to stop scary thoughts. Truth. Clarity. What if it was the landlord my forefinger was really pointing at in that courtroom? What that teacher was accused of was sort of like what Mr. Leigh did. Was I pointing at the idea of him? His nastiness or the curse he threw at me? I was six years old and had never heard the words "nigger" or "cunt" before, but the hate and revulsion in them didn't need definition. Just like later in school when other curses—with mysterious definitions but clear meanings—were hissed or shouted at me. Coon. Topsy. Clinkertop. Sambo. Ooga booga. Ape sounds and scratching of the sides, imitating zoo monkeys. One day a girl and three boys heaped a bunch of bananas on my desk and did their monkey imitations. They treated me like a freak, strange, soiling like a spill of ink on white paper. I didn't complain to the teacher for the same reason Sweetness cautioned me about Mr. Leigh—I might get suspended or even expelled.

So I let the name-calling, the bullying travel like poison, like lethal viruses through my veins, with no antibiotic available. Which, actually, was a good thing now I think of it, because I built up immunity so tough that not being a "nigger girl" was all I needed to win. I became a deep dark beauty who doesn't need Botox for kissable lips or tanning spas to hide a deathlike pallor. And I don't need silicon in my butt. I sold my elegant blackness to all those childhood ghosts and now they pay me for it. I have to say, forcing those tormentors—the real ones and others like them—to drool with envy when they see me is more than payback. It's glory.

Today is Monday or is it Tuesday? Anyway, I've been in and out of bed for two days. I've stopped worrying about my earlobes; I can always get them pierced again. Brooklyn telephones and keeps me up to date on office matters. I asked for and got an extension on my leave. She is "acting" regional manager now. Good for her. She deserves it just for getting me out of that Decagon catastrophe, taking care of me for days, seeing to the return of my Jaguar, hiring a cleaning crew, choosing the plastic surgeon. She even fired Rose, my maid, for me when I could no longer stand the sight of her—fat, with cantaloupe breasts and watermelon behind. I couldn't have healed without Brooklyn. Still, her calls are fewer and fewer.

Brooklyn

I thought he was a predator. I don't care how wild a dancing crowd is, you just don't grab somebody from behind
like that unless you know them. But she didn't mind at all.
She let him squeeze her, rub up against her and she didn't
know a thing about him, still doesn't. But I do. I saw him
with a bunch of raggedy losers at the subway entrance.
Panhandling, for Christ's sake. And once I'm pretty sure I
saw him sprawled on the steps of the library, pretending he
was reading a book so the cops wouldn't tell him to move
on. Another time I saw him sitting at a coffee shop table
writing in a notebook, trying to look serious, like he had
something important to do. It was surely him I saw walking aimlessly in neighborhoods far from Bride's apartment.
What was he doing there? Seeing another woman? Bride
never mentioned what he did, what, if any, job he had. Said
she liked the mystery. Liar. She liked the sex. Addicted to it
and believe me I know. When the three of us were together
she was different somehow. Confident, not so needy or constantly, obviously soliciting praise. In his company she shim-
mered, but quietly kind of. I don't know. Yes, he was one

good-looking man. So what? What else did he offer besides a rut between sheets? He didn't have a dime to his name.

I could have warned her. I'm not a bit surprised he left her like a skunk leaves a smell. If she knew what I knew she would have thrown him out. One day just for fun I flirted with him, tried to seduce him. In her own bedroom, mind you. I was bringing something to Bride, mock-ups of packaging. I have her key and just unlocked and opened the door. When I called her name, he answered saying, "She's not here." I went into her bedroom—there he was lying in her bed reading. Naked too, under a sheet that reached to his waist. On impulse, and it really was impulse, I dropped the package, kicked off my shoes and then like in a porn video the rest of my clothes slowly followed. He watched me closely while I stripped but didn't say a word so I knew he wanted me to stay. I never wear underthings so when I unzipped my jeans and kicked them away I simply stood there naked as a newborn. He just stared, but only at my face and so hard I blinked. I fingered my hair then joined him: slipped between the sheets; put my arm around his chest and planted light kisses there. He put his book away.

Between kisses, I whispered, "Don't you want another flower in your garden?"

He said, "Are you sure you know what makes a garden grow?"

"Sure do," I said. "Tenderness."

"And dung," he answered.

I elbowed myself up and stared at him. Bastard. He wasn't smiling but he wasn't pushing me away either. I jumped off the bed and picked up my clothes as quickly as I could. He didn't even watch me get dressed, asshole. He went back to reading his book. If I'd wanted to I could have made him make love to me. I really could have. I probably shouldn't have come on so sudden. Maybe if I had eased up a bit, slowed down. Taken it easy.

Well, anyway, Bride doesn't know a thing about her used-to-be lover. But I do.

Bride

I don't get it. Who the hell is he? His duffel bag, which I am determined to trash like the other one, is stuffed with more books, one in German, two books of poetry, one by somebody named Hass and some paperback books by more writers I've never heard of.

Christ. I thought I knew him. I know he has degrees from some university. He owns T-shirts that say so, but I never thought about that part of his life because what was important in our relationship, other than our lovemaking and his complete understanding of me, was the fun we had. Dancing in the clubs, other couples watching us with envy, boat rides with friends, hanging out on the beach. Finding these books prove how little I know about him, that he was somebody else, somebody thinking things he never talked about. True, our conversations were mostly about me but they were not the joke-filled, sarcastic ones I usually had with other men. To them, anything besides my flirting or their pronouncements would lead to disagreements, arguments, breakups. I could never have described my childhood to them as I did to Booker. Well, there were times when he talked to me at length, but none of it was intimate—it was more like a lecture. Once when we were at the shore stretched out in beach chairs, he started talking to me about the history of water in California. A bit boring, yes, and I was sort of interested. Still, I fell asleep.

I have no idea what occupied him when I was at the office and I never asked. I thought he liked me especially because I never probed, nagged or asked him about his past. I left him his private life. I thought it showed how much I trusted him—that it was him I was attracted to, not what he did. Every girl I know introduces her boyfriend as a lawyer or artist or club owner or broker or whatever. The job, not the guy, is what the girlfriend adores. "Bride, come meet Steve. He's a lawyer at—" "I'm dating this fabulous film producer—" "Joey is CFO at—" "My boyfriend got a part in that TV show—"

I shouldn't have—trusted him, I mean. I spilled my heart to him; he told me nothing about himself. I talked; he listened. Then he split, left without a word. Mocking me, dumping me exactly as Sofia Huxley did. Neither of us had mentioned marriage, but I really thought I had found my guy. "You not the woman" is the last thing I expected to hear.

Days, weeks of mail fill the basket on the table near my door. After searching the refrigerator for something to nibble on, I decide to examine the pile—toss out the pleas for money from every charity in the world, the promises of gifts from banks, stores and failing businesses. There are just two first-class letters. One is from Sweetness. "Hi, Honey," then stuff about her doctors' advice before the usual hint for money. The other is addressed to Booker Starbern from Salvatore Ponti on Seventeenth Street. I tear it open and find a reminder invoice. Sixty-eight dollars overdue. I don't know whether to trash the invoice or go see what Mr. Ponti did for sixty-eight dollars. Before I can make up my mind, the telephone rings.

"Hey, how was it? Last night. Fab, huh? You were a knockout, as usual." Brooklyn is slurping something be-tween words. A calorie-free, energy-filled, diet-supporting, fake-flavored, creamy, dye-colored something. "Wasn't that after-party the bomb?"

"Yeah," I answer.

"You don't sound sure. Did that guy you left with turn out to be Mr. Rogers or Superman? Who is he anyway?"

I go to my bedside table and look again at the note. "Phil something."

"How was he? I went to Rocco's with Billy and we—"

"Brooklyn, I have to get out of here. Away somewhere."

"What? You mean now?"

"Didn't we talk about a cruise somewhere?" My voice is whiny, I know.

"We did, sure, but after YOU, GIRL starts shipping.

The sample gift bags are in and the ad guys have several really cool ideas for . . ."

She rattles on until I stop her. "Look, I'll call you later. I'm a bit hung over."

"No kidding." Brooklyn giggles.

When I hang up I've already decided to check out Mr. Ponti's.

Sofia

I am not allowed to be near children. Home care was my first job after I was paroled. It suited me because the lady I cared for was nice. Grateful, even, for my help. And I liked being away from noise and a lot of people. Decagon is loud, packed with mistreated women and take-no-shit guards. My first week in Brookhaven, before being moved to Decagon, I watched an inmate get smacked across the back of her head with a belt just because she knocked her plate of food on the floor. The guard made her get down on all fours and eat it. She tried but started vomiting, so they took her to the infirmary. The food wasn't all that bad—corn pudding and Spam. I think she was probably sick with flu or something. Decagon is better than Brookhaven, where they loved to strip-search us at every exit and entrance, or just because. But still, at the second place there was always some prisoner-guard drama and when there wasn't, when we worked at our jobs, the noise, quarrels, fights, laughter, shouts went on and on. Even lights out just toned it down from a roar to a bark. At least I thought so. Quiet is mostly what I liked about being a home-care helper. After one month, though,

I had to quit because my patient's grandchildren visited her on weekends. My parole officer found me something similar but without children—a nursing home that didn't call itself a hospice but that is what it mostly was. At first I didn't like being around so many people in another institution, especially ones I had to answer to. But I got used to it since my superiors were not menacing me even though they wore uniforms. Anything that looked or felt like prison gave me a bad attitude.

Somehow I survived those fifteen years. Had it not been for weekend basketball games and Julie, my cellmate and only friend, I wonder if I would have made it. For the first two years we two, sentenced for child abuse, were avoided in the cafeteria. We were cursed and spit on, and the guards tossed our cell every now and then. After a while they mostly forgot about us. We were at the bottom of the heap of murderers, arsonists, drug dealers, bomb-throwing revolutionaries and the mentally ill. Hurting little children was their idea of the lowest of the low—which is a hoot since the drug dealers could care less about who they poison or how old they were and the arsonists didn't separate the children from the families they burned. And bomb throwers are not selective or known for precision. If anybody doubted their hatred of me and Julie all they had to do was notice how the love of children was posted everywhere—pictures of babies and kids were all over the cell walls. Anybody's kid would do.

Julie was serving time for smothering her disabled daughter. The little girl's photograph was posted on the wall above her bed. Molly. Big head, slack mouth, the loveliest blue eyes in the world. Julie whispered to Molly's photo at night or whenever she could. Not asking for forgiveness, but telling her dead daughter stories—fairy tales, mostly, all about princesses. I never told her, but I liked those stories too—helped me sleep. We worked in the sewing shop, making uniforms for a medical company that paid us twelve cents an hour. When my fingers got too stiff to work the machine properly, I was moved to the kitchen where I dropped whatever food I didn't scorch and was sent back to the sewing machines. But Julie wasn't there. She was in the infirmary after trying to hang herself. She didn't know how. A few of the cruelest inmates offered to show her. When she returned to population she was different—quiet, sad and not much company. I guess it was the gang rape by four women, then later the loving enslavement she was in with one of the elderly women—a husband called Lover whom no one trifled with. Nobody, guards or inmates, liked me enough to want more than a casual hookup. I was a fighter and too tall, I guess, almost a giant in that place. Fine, I thought—the less licking the better.

In all those years I received exactly two letters from Jack, my husband. The first was a Dear Honey letter that turned into complaints like "I'm being [blacked-out word] here." Beaten? Fucked? Tortured? What other word would the prison mail censor deny? The second letter began, "What the hell were you thinking, bitch?" No blacked-out word there. I didn't answer. My parents sent me packages at Christmas and on my birthday: nutritious candy bars, tampons, religious pamphlets and socks. But they never wrote, called or visited. I wasn't surprised. They were always hard to please. The family Bible was placed on a stand right next to the piano, where my mother played hymns after supper. They never said so, but I suspect they were glad to be rid of me. In their world of God and Devil no innocent person is sentenced to prison.

I mostly did what I was told. And I read a lot. That was one good thing about Decagon—its library. Since real public libraries don't need or want books anymore, they send them to prisons and old-folks' homes. Anything other than religious tracts and the Bible were banned in my family's home. As a teacher I thought I was well read although in college, as an education major, I was not required to read any literature. Until I was in prison I'd never read *The Odyssey* or Jane Austen. None of it taught me much, but concentrating on escapes, deceits, and who would marry whom was a welcome distraction.

In the taxicab on the first day of my parole I felt like a little kid seeing the world for the first time—houses surrounded by grass so green it hurt my eyes. The flowers seemed to be painted because I didn't remember roses that shade of lavender or sunflowers so blindingly bright. Everything seemed not just remodeled but brand-new. When I rolled down the window to smell the fresh air, the wind caught my hair—whipping it backward and sideways. That's when I knew I was free. Wind. Wind fingering, stroking, kissing my hair.

That same day one of the students who testified against me—all grown up now—knocked on the door. I was in a sleazy motel room desperate to eat and sleep in solitude for once. No petty arguments or sex grunts, loud sobs or snores from nearby cells. I don't think many people appreciate silence or realize that it is as close to music as you can get. Quiet makes some folks fidget or feel too lonely. After fifteen years of noise I was hungry for silence more than food. So I gobbled everything, puked it up and was just about to get some deep solitude when I heard banging on the door.

I didn't know who she was although something about her eyes seemed familiar. In another world her black skin would have been remarkable, but living all those years in Decagon it wasn't. After fifteen years of wearing ugly flat shoes, I was more interested in her fashionable ones—alligator or snakeskin, pointy toes and heels so high they were like the stilts of circus clowns. She spoke as if we were friends but I didn't know what she was talking about or what she wanted until she threw money at me. She was one of the students who testified against me, one of the ones who helped kill me, take my life away. How could she think cash would erase fifteen years of life as death? I blanked. My fists took over as I thought I was battling the Devil. Exactly the one my mother always talked about— seductive but evil. As soon as I threw her out and got rid of her Satan's disguise, I curled up into a ball on the bed and waited for the police. Waited and waited. None came. If they had bashed in the door they would have seen a woman finally broken down after fifteen years of staying strong. For the first time after all those years, I cried. Cried and cried and cried until I fell asleep. When I woke up I reminded myself that freedom is never free. You have to fight for it. Work for it and make sure you are able to handle it.

Now I think of it, that black girl did do me a favor. Not the foolish one she had in mind, not the money she offered, but the gift that neither of us planned: the release of tears unshed for fifteen years. No more bottling up. No more filth. Now I am clean and able.

PART II

❦

A taxi was preferable because parking a Jaguar in that neighborhood was as dim-witted as it was risky. That Booker frequented this part of the city startled Bride. Why here? she wondered. There were music shops in unthreatening neighborhoods, places where tattooed men and young girls dressed like ghouls weren't huddled on corners or squatting on curbs.

Once the driver stopped at the address she'd given him, and after he told her, "Sorry, lady. I can't wait here for you," Bride stepped quickly toward the door of Salvatore Ponti's Pawn and Repair Palace. Inside it was clear that the word "Palace" was less a mistake than an insanity. Under dusty glass counters row after row of jewelry and watches crouched. A man, good-looking the way elderly men can be, moved down the counter toward her. His jeweler's eyes swept all he could take in of his customer.

"Mr. Ponti?"

"Call me Sally, sweetheart. What can I do you for?"

Bride waved the overdue notice and explained she'd come to settle the bill and pick up whatever had been repaired. Sally examined the notice. "Oh, yeah," he said. "Thumb ring. Mouthpiece. They're in back. Come on."

Together they went into a back room where guitars and horns hung on the walls and all sorts of metal pieces covered the cloth of a table. The man working there looked up from his magnifying glass to examine Bride and then the notice. He went to a cupboard and removed a trumpet wrapped in purple cloth.

"He didn't mention the pinkie ring," said the repairman, "but I gave him one anyway. Picky guy, real picky."

Bride took the horn thinking she didn't even know Booker owned one or played it. Had she been interested she would have known that that was what caused the dark dimple on his upper lip. She handed Sally the amount owed.

"Nice, though, and smart for a country boy," said the repairman.

"Country boy?" Bride frowned. "He's not from the country. He lives here."

"Oh, yeah? Told me he was from some hick town up north," said Sally.

"Whiskey," said the repairman.

"What are you talking about?" asked Bride.

"Funny, right? Who could forget a town called Whiskey? Nobody, that's who."

The men burst into snorts of laughter and started calling

out other memorable names of towns: Intercourse, Pennsylvania; No Name, Colorado; Hell, Michigan; Elephant Butte, New Mexico; Pig, Kentucky; Tightwad, Missouri. Exhausted, finally, by their mutual amusement, they turned their attention back to the customer.

"Look here," said Sally. "He gave us another address. A forward." He flipped through his Rolodex. "Ha. Somebody named Olive. Q. Olive. Whiskey, California."

"No street address?"

"Come on, honey. Who says they have streets in a town called Whiskey?" Sally was having a good time keeping himself amused as well as keeping the pretty black girl in his shop. "Deer tracks maybe," he added.

Bride left the shop quickly, but realized just as quickly that there were no roaming cabs. She was forced to return and ask Sally to phone one for her.

Sofia

I ought to be sad. Daddy called my supervisor to say Mommy died. I asked for an advance to buy a ticket to fly out for the funeral, assuming my parole officer would let me. I remember every inch of the church where the funeral would be held. The wooden Bible holders on the backs of the pews, the greenish light from the window behind Reverend Walker's head. And the smell—perfume, tobacco and something more. Godliness, perhaps. Clean, upright and very good for you like the dining room corner in Mommy's house. The blue-and-white wallpaper I came to know better than my own face. Roses, lilacs, clematis all shades of blue against snowy white. I stood there, sometimes for two hours; a quiet scolding, a punishment for something I don't remember now or even then. I wet my underwear? I played "wrestle" with a neighbor's son? I couldn't wait to get out of Mommy's house and marry the first man who asked. Two years with him was the same—obedience, silence, a bigger blue-and-white corner. Teaching was the only pleasure I had.

I have to admit, though, that Mommy's rules, her strict

discipline helped me survive in Decagon. Until the first day of my release, that is, when I blew. Really blew. I beat up that black girl who testified against me. Beating her, kicking and punching her freed me up more than being paroled. I felt I was ripping blue-and-white wallpaper, returning slaps and running the devil Mommy knew so well out of my life.

I wonder what happened to her. Why she didn't call the police. Her eyes, frozen with fear, delighted me then. The next morning with my face bloated from hours of sobbing, I opened the door. Thin streaks of blood were on the pavement and a pearl earring nearby. Maybe it belonged to her, maybe not. Anyway I kept it. It's still in my wallet as what? A kind of remembrance? When I tend to my patients—put their teeth back in their mouths, rub their behinds, their thighs to limit bed sores, or when I sponge their lacy skin before lotioning it, in my mind I am putting the black girl back together, healing her, thanking her. For the release.

Sorry Mommy.

꧁

The sun and the moon shared the horizon in a distant friendship, each unfazed by the other. Bride didn't notice the light, how carnival it made the sky. The shaving brush and razor were packed in the trumpet case and stowed in the trunk. She thought about both until she became distracted by the music on the Jaguar's radio. Nina Simone was too aggressive, making Bride think of something other than herself. She switched to soft jazz, more suitable for the car's leather interior as well as a soothing background for the anxiety she needed to tamp down. She had never done anything this reckless. The reason for this tracking was not love, she knew; it was more hurt than anger that made her drive into unknown territory to locate the one person she once trusted, who made her feel safe, colonized somehow. Without him the world was more than confusing—shallow, cold, deliberately hostile. Like the atmosphere in her mother's house where she never knew the right thing to do or say or remember what the rules were. Leave the spoon in the cereal bowl or place it next to the bowl; tie her shoelaces with a bow or a double knot; fold her socks down or pull them straight up to the calf? What were the rules and when did they change? When she soiled the bedsheet with her first menstrual blood, Sweetness slapped her and then pushed her into a tub of cold water. Her shock was alleviated by the satisfaction of being touched, handled by a mother who avoided physical contact whenever possible.

How could he? Why would he leave her stripped of all comfort, emotional security? Yes, her quick response to his exit was silly, stupid. Like the taunt of a third grader who had no clue about life.

He was part of the pain—not a savior at all, and now her life was in shambles because of him. The pieces of it that she had stitched together: personal glamour, control in an exciting even creative profession, sexual freedom and most of all a shield that protected her from any overly intense feeling, be it rage, embarrassment or love. Her response to physical attack was no less cowardly than her reaction to a sudden, unexplained breakup. The first produced tears; the second a flip "Yeah, so?" Being beaten up by Sofia was like Sweetness's slap without the pleasure of being touched. Both confirmed her helplessness in the presence of confounding cruelty.

Too weak, too scared to defy Sweetness, or the landlord, or Sofia Huxley, there was nothing in the world left to do but stand up for herself finally and confront the first man she had bared her soul to, unaware that he was mocking her. It would take courage though, something that, being successful in her career, she thought she had plenty of. That and exotic beauty.

According to the men at Sally's he was from a place called Whiskey. Maybe he had gone back there. Maybe not. He could be living with Miss Q. Olive, another woman he didn't want, or he might have moved on. Whatever the case, Bride would track him, force him to explain why she didn't deserve better treatment from him, and second, what did he mean by "not the woman"? Who? This here woman? This one driving a Jaguar in an oyster-white cashmere dress and boots of brushed rabbit fur the color of the moon? The beautiful one, according to everybody with two eyes, who runs a major department in a billion-dollar company? The one who was already imagining newer product lines—eyelashes, for example. In addition to breasts, every woman (his kind or not) wanted longer, thicker eyelashes. A woman could be cobra-thin and starving, but if she had grapefruit boobs and raccoon eyes, she was deliriously happy. Right. She would get right on it after this trip.

The highway became less and less crowded as she drove east and then north. Soon, she imagined, forests would edge the road watching her, as trees always did. In a few hours she would be in north valley country: logging camps, hamlets no older than she was, dirt roads as old as the Tribes. As long as she was on a state highway, she decided to look for a diner, eat and freshen up before driving into territory too sparse for comfort. A collection of signs on a single billboard advertised one brand of gas, four of food, two of lodging. Three miles on, Bride left the highway and turned in to the oasis. The diner she chose was spotless and empty. The smell of beer and tobacco was not recent, nor was the framed Confederate flag that nestled the official American one.

"Yeah?" The counter waitress's eyes were wide and roving. Bride was used to that look, as well as the open mouth that accompanied it. It reminded her of the reception she got on the first days of school. Shock, as though she had three eyes.

"May I have a white omelet, no cheese?"

"White? You mean no eggs?"

"No. No yolks."

Bride ate as much as she could of that redneck version of digestible food, then asked where the ladies' room was. She left a five-dollar bill on the counter in case the waitress thought she was skipping. In the bathroom she confirmed that there was still reason to be alarmed by her hairless pudenda. Then standing at the mirror over the sink, she noticed the neckline of her cashmere dress was askew, slanting down so much her left shoulder was bare. Adjusting it, she saw that the shoulder slide was due neither to poor posture nor to a manufacturing flaw. The top of the dress sagged as if instead of a size 2 she had purchased a 4 and just now noticed the difference. But the dress had fit her perfectly when she started this trip. Perhaps, she thought, there was a defect in the cloth or the design; otherwise she was losing weight—fast. Not a problem. No such thing as too thin in her business. She would simply choose clothes more carefully. A scary memory of altered earlobes shook her but she dared not connect it to other alterations to her body.

While collecting the change and deciding on the tip, Bride asked directions to Whiskey.

"Ain't all that far," said the bug-eyed, smirking waitress. "A hundred miles, maybe one fifty. You'll make it before dark."

Is that what backwoods trash called "not far"? wondered Bride. One hundred and fifty miles? She gassed up, had the tires checked and followed the loop away from the oasis back onto the highway. Contrary to the waitress's certainty, it was very dark by the time she saw the exit marked not by a number but a name—Whiskey Road.

At least it was paved, narrow and curvy but still paved. Perhaps that was the reason she trusted the high-beam headlights and accelerated. She never saw it coming. The automobile overshot a sharp bend in the road and crashed into what must have been the world's first and biggest tree, which was circled by bushes hiding its lower trunk. Bride fought the air bag, moving so fast and in such panic she did not notice her foot caught and twisted in the space between the brake pedal and the buckled door, until trying to free it flattened her with pain. She managed to unbuckle the seat belt but nothing else helped. She lay there awkwardly on the driver's seat, trying to ease her left foot out of the elegant rabbit-furred boot. Her efforts proved both painful and impossible. Stretching and twisting, she managed to get to her cellphone, but its face was blank except for the "no service" message. The likelihood of a passing car was dim in the dark but possible, so she pressed the car's horn, desperate for the honk, to do more than frighten owls. It frightened nothing because it made no sound. There was nothing she could do but lie there the rest of the night, by turns afraid, angry, in pain, weepy. The moon was a toothless grin and even the stars, seen through the tree limb that had fallen like a throttling arm across the windshield, frightened her. The piece of sky she could glimpse was a dark carpet of gleaming knives pointed at her and aching to be released. She felt world-hurt—an awareness of malign forces changing her from a courageous adventurer into a fugitive.

The sun merely hinted at its rise, an apricot slice teasing the sky with a promise of revealing its whole self. Bride, whipped by body cramp and leg pain, felt a tingle of hope along with the dawn. A helmetless motorcyclist, a truck full of loggers, a serial rapist, a boy on a bike, a bear hunter— was there no one to lend a hand? While imagining who or what might rescue her, a small bone-white face appeared at the passenger's side window. A girl, very young, carrying a black kitten, stared at her with the greenest eyes Bride had ever seen.

"Help me. Please. Help me." Bride would have screamed but she didn't have the strength.

The girl watched her for a long, long time, then turned away and disappeared.

"Oh, God," Bride whispered. Was she hallucinating? If not, surely the girl had gone for help. Nobody, not the mentally disabled or the genetically violent, would leave her there. Would they? Suddenly, as they hadn't in the dark, the surrounding trees coming alive in the dawn really scared her, and the silence was terrifying. She decided to turn on the ignition, shift into reverse and blast the Jaguar out of there—foot or no foot. Just as she turned the ignition key to the withering sound of a dead battery a man appeared. Bearded with long blond hair and slit black eyes. Rape? Murder? Bride trembled, watching him squint at her through the window. Then he left. What seemed to Bride like hours were only a few minutes before he returned with a saw and a crowbar. Swallowing and stiff with fear she watched him saw the branch from the hood then, taking a vise from his back pocket, pry and yank the door open. Bride's scream of pain startled the green-eyed girl standing by who watched the scene with her mouth open. Carefully the man eased Bride's foot from under the brake pedal and away from the car's smashed door. His hair hung forward as he lifted her out of the car seat. Silently, asking no questions and offering no verbal comfort, he positioned her in his arms. With the emerald-eyed girl tagging along, he carried Bride half a mile down a sandy path leading to a warehouse-looking structure that might serve a killer as a house. Enclosed in his arms and in unrelenting pain, she said, "Don't hurt me, please don't hurt me," over and over before fainting.

"Why is her skin so black?"

"For the same reason yours is so white."

"Oh. You mean like my kitten?"

"Right. Born that way."

Bride sucked her teeth. What an easy conversation between mother and daughter. She was faking sleep, eaves-dropping under a Navajo blanket, her ankle propped on a pillow, throbbing with pain in its furry boot. The rescuing man had brought Bride to this sort-of house, and instead of raping and torturing her, asked his wife to look after her while he took the truck. He wasn't sure, he said, but there was a chance it wasn't too early for the only doctor in the area to be found. He didn't think it was just a sprain, the bearded man said. The ankle might be broken. Without phone service, he had no choice but to get in his truck and drive into the village for the doctor.

"My name is Evelyn," said the wife. "My husband's is Steve. Yours?"

"Bride. Just Bride." For the first time her concocted name didn't sound hip. It sounded Hollywoody, teenagey. That is until Evelyn motioned to the emerald-eyed girl. "Bride, this is Raisin. Actually we named her Rain because that is where we found her, but she prefers to call herself Raisin."

"Thank you, Raisin. You saved my life. Really." Bride, grateful for another vanity name, let a tear sting its way down her cheek. Evelyn gave her one of her husband's plaid, lumberjack shirts after helping her undress.

"Can I fix you some breakfast? Oatmeal?" she asked. "Or some warm bread and butter. You must have been trapped in there all night."

Bride declined, sweetly, she hoped. She just wanted to take a nap.

Evelyn tucked the blanket around her guest, mindful of the propped-up leg, and did not trouble to whisper the black or white kitten conversation as she moved toward the sink. She was a tall woman with unfashionable hips and a long chestnut braid swinging down her back. She reminded Bride of someone she had seen in the movies, not a recent one but something made in the forties or fifties when film stars had distinguishing faces unlike now, when hairstyles alone separated one star from another. But she could not put a name to the memory—actress or film. Little Raisin, on the other hand, resembled no one Bride had ever seen— milk-white skin, ebony hair, neon eyes, undetermined age.

What had Evelyn said? "That is where we found her"? In the rain.

Steve and Evelyn's house seemed to be a converted studio or machine shop: one large space, containing table, chairs, sink, wood-burning cook stove and the scratchy couch Bride lay on. Against a wall stood a loom with small baskets of yarn nearby. Above was a skylight that needed a good power-cleaning. All over the room, light, unaided by electricity, moved like water—a shadow here could be gone in an instant, a shaft hitting a copper pot might take minutes to dissolve. An open door to the rear revealed a room where two beds, one of rope, another of iron, stood. Something meaty, like chicken, roasted in the oven while Evelyn and the girl chopped mushrooms and green peppers at the rough home-made table. Without warning they began to sing some dumb old hippie song.

"This land is your land, this land is my land . . ."

Bride quickly dashed a bright memory of Sweetness humming some blues song while washing panty hose in the sink, little Lula Ann hiding behind the door to hear her. How nice it would have been if mother and daughter could have sung together. Embracing that dream, she did fall into a deep sleep, only to be awakened around noon by booming male voices. Steve, accompanied by a very old, rumpled doctor, clumped into the house.

"This is Walt," said Steve. He stood near the couch, showing something close to a smile.

"Dr. Muskie," said the doctor. "Walter Muskie, MD, PhD, LLD, DDT, OMB."

Steve laughed. "He's joking."

"Hello," said Bride, looking back and forth from her foot to the doctor's face. "I hope it's not too bad."

"We'll see," answered Dr. Muskie.

Bride sucked air through clenched teeth as the doctor sliced through her elegant white boot. Expertly and without empathy he examined her ankle and announced it fractured at the least and unfixable here in Steve's house—she needed to go to the clinic for an X-ray, cast and so on. All he could do, or would do, is clean and bind it so its swell wouldn't worsen.

Bride refused to go. She was suddenly so hungry it made her angry. She wanted to bathe and then eat before being driven to another tacky rural clinic. Meantime she asked Dr. Muskie for painkillers.

"No," said Steve. "No way. First things first. Besides, we don't have all day."

Steve carried her to his truck, squeezed her between himself and the doctor and took off. Two hours later as the two of them drove back from the clinic she had to admit the splint had eased her pain, as had the pills. Whiskey Clinic was across the street from a post office on the first floor of a charming sea-blue clapboard house, which also contained a barbershop. Windows on the second floor advertised used clothes. Quaint, thought Bride, expecting to be helped into an equally quaint examination room. To her surprise the equipment was as cutting edge as her plastic surgeon's.

Dr. Muskie smiled at her astonishment. "Loggers are like soldiers," he said. "They have the worst wounds and need the best and quickest care."

After examining the screen-shot from a sonogram, Dr. Muskie told her she would live but she would probably need a month at the least to heal—maybe six weeks. "Syndesmosis," he said to his uncomprehending patient. "Between the fibula and the tibia. Maybe surgery—probably not, if you do what I say."

He put her ankle in a splint, saying he would give her a cast when the swelling decreased. And she would have to come back to his office for it.

An hour later she was back in the truck sitting next to a silent Steve with her left leg sticking as straight under the dashboard as the splint allowed. After being carried back to the house, Bride found that her earlier hunger had dissipated as the awareness of being unwashed and sour-smelling overwhelmed her.

"I'd like to take a bath, please," she said.

"We don't have a bathroom," said Evelyn. "I can sponge you for now. When your ankle is ready, I'll heat water for the washtub."

Slop jar, outhouse toilet, metal washtub, broke-down scratchy couch for a month? Bride started to cry, and they let her while Rain and Evelyn went on preparing a meal.

Later, after the family finished eating, Bride tried to overcome her embarrassment and accepted a basin of cold water to rinse her face and armpits. Then she roused herself enough to smile and take the plate Evelyn held before her. Quail, as it turned out, not chicken, with thick mushroom gravy. Following the meal, Bride felt more than embarrassed; she was ashamed—crying every minute, petulant, childish and unwilling to help herself or accept aid gracefully from others. Here she was among people living the barest life, putting themselves out for her without hesitation, asking nothing in return. Yet, as was often the case, her gratitude and embarrassment were short-lived. They were treating her like a stray cat or a dog with a broken leg that they felt sorry for. Sullen and picking at her fingernails, she asked Evelyn whether she had a nail file or any nail polish. Evelyn grinned and held up her own hands without speaking. Point taken—Evelyn's hands were less for holding the stem of a wineglass and more for chopping kindling and wringing the necks of chickens. Who are these people, wondered Bride, and where did they come from? They hadn't asked her where she was from or where she was going. They simply tended her, fed her, arranged for her car to be towed for repair. It was too hard, too strange for her to understand the kind of care they offered—free, without judgment or even a passing interest in who she was or where she was going. She wondered on occasion if they were planning something. Something bad.

But the days passed with boredom unbroken. Steve and Evelyn occasionally spent time after supper sitting outside singing songs by the Beatles or Simon and Garfunkel— Steve strumming his guitar, Evelyn joining him in tuneless soprano. Their laughter tinkling between wrong lines and missed notes.

In the following weeks of more visits to the clinic, leg exercises and waiting for the Jaguar to be repaired, Bride learned that her hosts were in their fifties. Steve had graduated from Reed College, Evelyn from Ohio State. With constant bursts of laughter they described how they met. First in India (Bride saw the light of pleasant memories shining in the looks they exchanged), then London, again in Berlin. Finally in Mexico they agreed to stop meeting that way (Steve touched Evelyn's cheek with his knuckle) so they got married in Tijuana and "moved to California to live a real life."

Bride's envy watching them was infantile but she couldn't stop herself. "By 'real' you mean poor?" She smiled to hide the sneer.

"What does 'poor' mean? No television?" Steve raised his eyebrows.

"It means no money," said Bride.

"Same thing," he answered. "No money, no television."

"Means no washing machine, no fridge, no bathroom, no money!"

"Money get you out of that Jaguar? Money save your ass?"

Bride blinked but was smart enough to say nothing. What did she know anyway about good for its own sake, or love without things?

She stayed with them for six difficult weeks, waiting until she could walk and her car was repaired. Apparently the single automobile-repair place had to send away for hinges or a completely new door for the Jaguar. Sleeping in a house of such deep darkness at night felt to Bride like being in a coffin. Outside the sky would be loaded with more stars than she had ever seen before. But in here under a filthy skylight and no electricity she had a problem sleeping.

Finally Dr. Muskie returned to remove her cast and give her a removable foot brace so she could limp about. She glimpsed the disgusting skin that had been hidden underneath the cast and shivered. Even more than having the cast removed, the best thing was Evelyn, true to her word, pouring pail after pail of hot water into a zinc tub. Then she handed Bride a sponge, a towel and a bar of hard-to-lather brown soap. After weeks of bird-washing Bride sank into the water with gratitude, prolonging the soaping until the water had cooled completely. It was when she stood to dry herself that she discovered that her chest was flat. Completely flat, with only the nipples to prove it was not her back. Her shock was so great she plopped back down into the dirty water, holding the towel over her chest like a shield.

I must be sick, dying, she thought. She plastered the wet towel above the place where her breasts had once upon a time announced themselves and risen to the lips of moaning lovers. Fighting panic she called out to Evelyn.

"Please, do you have something I can wear?"

"Sure," said Evelyn, and after a few minutes brought Bride a T-shirt and a pair of her own jeans. She said nothing about Bride's chest or the wet towel. She simply left her to get dressed in private. When Bride called her back saying the jeans were too large to stay on her hips, Evelyn exchanged them for a pair of Rain's, which fit Bride perfectly. When did I get so small? she wondered.

She meant to lie down just for a minute, to quiet the terror, collect her thoughts and figure out what was happening to her shrinking body, but without any drowsiness or warning she fell asleep. There out of that dark void sprang a vivid, fully felt dream. Booker's hand was moving between her thighs, and when her arms flew up and closed over his back he extracted his fingers, and slid between her legs what they called the pride and wealth of nations. She started to whisper or moan but his lips were pressing hers. She wrapped her legs around his rocking hips as though to slow them or help them or keep them there. Bride woke up moist and humming. Yet when she touched the place where her breasts used to be the humming changed to sobs. That's when she understood that the body changes began not simply after he left, but because he left.

Stay still, she thought; her brain was wobbly but she would straighten it, go about as if everything was normal. No one must know and no one must see. Her conversation and activity must be routine, like an after-bath washing of hair. Limping to the kitchen sink she poured water from the standing pitcher into a bowl, soaped then rinsed her hair. As she looked around for a dry towel Evelyn came in.

"Ooh, Bride," she said, smiling. "You got too much hair for a dish towel. Come on, let's sit outside and we can dry it in sunlight and fresh air."

"Okay, sure," said Bride. Acting normal was important, she thought. It might even restore the body changes—or halt them. She followed Evelyn to a rusty iron bench sitting in the yard bathed in bright platinum light. Next to it was a side table where a tin of marijuana and a bottle of unlabeled liquor sat. Toweling Bride's hair, Evelyn chatted away in typical beauty-parlor mode. How happy living here under stars with a perfect man made her, how much she had learned traveling, housekeeping without modern amenities, which she called trash-ready junk since none of it lasted, and how Rain had improved their lives.

When Bride asked her when and where Rain came from, Evelyn sat down and poured some of the liquor into a cup.

"It took a while to get the whole story," she said. Bride listened intently. Anything. Anything to stop thinking first about how her body was changing and second how to make sure no one noticed. When Evelyn handed her the T-shirt as she stepped out of the tub, Evelyn didn't notice or say a word. Bride had spectacular breasts when rescued from the Jaguar; she had them in Whiskey Clinic. Now they were gone, like a botched mastectomy that left nipples intact. Nothing hurt; her organs worked as usual except for a strangely delayed menstrual period. So what kind of illness was she suffering? One that was both visible and invisible. Him, she thought. His curse.

"Want some?" Evelyn pointed to the tin box.

"Yeah, okay." She watched Evelyn's expertise and took the result with gratitude. She coughed with the first toke, but none thereafter.

They were silently smoking for a while until Bride said, "Tell me what you meant by finding her in the rain."

"We did. Steve and I were driving home from some protest, I forget what, and saw this little girl, sopping wet on a brick doorstep. We had an old Volkswagen back then and he slowed down, then put on the brakes. Both of us thought she was lost or her door key was. He parked, got out and went to see what was the matter. First he asked her name."

"What did she say?"

"Nothing. Not a word. Drenched as she was, she turned her head away when Steve squatted down in front of her, but wow! when he touched her on her shoulder she jumped up and ran splashing off in wet tennis shoes. So he just got back in the car so we could continue our drive home. But then rain started really coming down—so hard we had trouble seeing through the windshield. So we called it quits and parked near a diner. Bruno's, it was called. Anyway, rather than wait in the car we went inside, more for shelter than for the coffee we ordered."

"So you lost her?"

"Then, yes." Evelyn, having exhausted the joint, replenished her cup and sipped from it.

"Did she come back?"

"No, but when the rain let up and we left the diner, I spotted her hunched up next to a Dumpster in the alley behind the building."

"Jesus," said Bride, shuddering as though it were she herself in that alley.

"It was Steve who decided not to leave her there. I wasn't so sure it was any of our business but he just went over and grabbed her, threw her over his shoulder. She was screaming, 'Kidnap! Kidnap!' but not too loud. I don't think she wanted attention, especially from pigs, I mean cops. We pushed her into the backseat, got in and locked the doors."

"Did she quiet down?"

"Oh no. She kept hollering 'Let me out,' and kicking the back of our seats. I tried to talk to her in a soft voice so she wouldn't be frightened of us. I said, 'You're soaking wet, honey.' She said, 'It's raining, bitch.' I asked her if her mother knew she was sitting outside in the rain and she said, 'Yeah, so?' I didn't know what to do with that answer. Then she started cursing—nastier words in a little kid's mouth you couldn't imagine."

"Really?"

"Steve and I looked at each other and without talking we decided what to do—get her dry, cleaned and fed, then try to find out where she belonged."

"You said she was about six when you found her?" asked Bride.

"I guess. I don't really know. She never said and I doubt she knows. Her baby teeth were gone when we took her. And so far she has never had a period and her chest is flat as a skateboard."

Bride shot up. Just the mention of a flat chest yanked her back to her problem. Had her ankle not prohibited it, she would have run, rocketed away from the scary suspicion that she was changing back into a little black girl.

One night and a day later Bride had calmed down a little. Since no one had noticed or commented on the changes in her body, how flat the T-shirt hung on her chest, the unpierced earlobes. Only she knew about unshaved but absent armpit and pubic hair. So all of this might be a hallucination, like the vivid dreams she was having when she managed to fall asleep. Or were they? Twice at night she woke to find Rain standing over her or squatting nearby—not threatening, just looking. But when she spoke to the girl, she seemed to disappear.

Helpless, idle. It became clear to Bride why boredom was so fought against. Without distraction or physical activity, the mind shuffled pointless, scattered recollections around and around. Focused worry would have been an improvement over disconnected, rags of thought. Minus the limited coherence of a dream, her mind moved from the condition of her fingernails to the time she walked into a lamppost, from judging a celebrity's gown to the state of her own teeth. She was stuck in a place so primitive it didn't even have a radio while watching a couple going about their daily chores—gardening, cleaning, cooking, weaving, mowing grass, chopping wood, canning. There was no one to talk to, at least not about anything she was interested in. Her determined refusal to think about Booker invariably collapsed. What if she couldn't find him? What if he's not with Mr. or Ms. Olive? Nothing would be right if the hunt she was on failed. And if it succeeded what would she do or say? Except for Sylvia, Inc., and Brooklyn, she felt she had been scorned and rejected by everybody all her life. Booker was the one person she was able to confront—which was the same as confronting herself, standing up for herself. Wasn't she worth something? Anything?

She missed Brooklyn whom she thought of as her only true friend: loyal, funny, generous. Who else would drive miles to find her after that bloody horror at a cheap motel then take such good care of her? It wasn't fair, she thought, to leave her in the dark as to where she was. Of course she couldn't tell her friend the reason for her flight. Brooklyn would have tried to dissuade her, or worse, taunt and laugh at her. Persuade her how ill-advised and reckless the idea was. Nevertheless, the right thing to do was to contact her.

Since she couldn't call, Bride decided to drop her a note. When asked, Evelyn said she didn't have any stationery but she offered Bride a sheet of the tablet paper used to teach Rain to write. Evelyn promised she would get Steve to mail it.

Bride was expert at company memos but not personal letters. What should she say?

I'm okay, so far . . . ?

Sorry to leave without telling . . . ?

I have to do this on my own because . . . ?

When she put down the pencil she examined her fingernails.

Usually the sound of Evelyn's weaving at the loom soothed her, but this day the click, knock, click, knock of the shuttle and pedal was extremely irritating. Whatever road her thoughts traveled, the possibility of shame waited at the end. Suppose Booker wasn't living in a town called Whiskey. And if he was, what then? What if he was with another woman? What did she have to say to him anyhow, besides "I hate you for what you did" or "Please come back to me"? Maybe she could find a way to hurt him, really hurt him. Muddled as her thoughts were, they coalesced around one necessity—an unrelenting need to confront him, regardless of the outcome. Annoyed and irritated by the "what-ifs" and the sound of Evelyn's loom, she decided to hobble outside. She opened the door and called, "Rain, Rain."

The girl was lying in the grass watching a trail of ants going about their civilized business.

"What?" Rain looked up.

"Want to go for a walk?"

"What for?" By the tone of her voice it was clear the ants were far more interesting than Bride's company.

"I don't know," said Bride.

That answer seemed to please. She jumped up smiling and brushing her shorts. "Okay, if you wanna."

The quiet between them was easy at first as each appeared to be deep in her own thoughts. Bride limping, Rain skipping or dawdling along the verge of bushes and grass. Half a mile down the road Rain's husky voice broke the silence.

"They stole me."

"Who? You mean Steve and Evelyn?" Bride stopped and watched Rain scratch the back of her calf. "They said they found you, sitting in the rain."

"Yep."

"So why did you say 'stole'?"

"Because I didn't ask them to take me and they didn't ask if I wanted to go."

"Then why did you?"

"I was wet, freezing too. Evelyn gave me a blanket and a box of raisins to eat."

"Are you sorry they took you?" I guess not, thought Bride—otherwise you would have run away.

"Oh, no. Never. This is the best place. Besides there's no place else to go." Rain yawned and rubbed her nose.

"You mean you don't have a home?"

"I used to but my mother lives there."

"So you ran away."

"No I didn't. She threw me out. Said 'Get the fuck out.' So I did."

"Why? Why would she do that?" Why would anybody do that to a child? Bride wondered. Even Sweetness, who for years couldn't bear to look at or touch her, never threw her out.

"Because I bit him."

"Bit who?"

"Some guy. A regular. One of the ones she let do it to me. Oh, look. Blueberries!" Rain was searching through roadside bushes.

"Wait a minute," Bride said. "Do what to you?"

"He stuck his pee thing in my mouth and I bit it. So she apologized to him, gave back his twenty-dollar bill and made me stand outside." The berries were bitter, not the wild sweet stuff she expected. "She wouldn't let me back in.

I kept pounding on the door. She opened it once to throw me my sweater." Rain spit the last bit of blueberry into the dirt.

As Bride imagined the scene her stomach fluttered. How could anybody do that to a child, any child, and one's own? "If you saw your mother again what would you say to her?"

Rain grinned. "Nothing. I'd chop her head off."

"Oh, Rain. You don't mean that."

"Yes I do. I used to think about it a lot. How it would look—her eyes, her mouth, the blood shooting out of her neck. Made me feel good just thinking about it."

A smooth ridge of rock jutted parallel to the road. Bride took Rain's hand and led her gently to the stone. They both sat down. Neither saw the doe and her fawn standing among the trees on the other side of the road. The doe watching the pair of humans was as still as the tree she stood next to. The fawn nestled her flank.

"Tell me," said Bride. "Tell me."

At the sound of Bride's voice, mother and child fled.

"Come on, Rain." Bride put her hand on Rain's knee. "Tell me."

And she did, her emerald eyes sometimes sparkling wide other times narrowed to dark olive slits as she described the savvy, the perfect memory, the courage needed for street life. You had to find out where the public toilets were, she said; how to avoid children's services, police, how to escape drunks, dope heads. But knowing where sleep was safe was the most important thing. It took time and she had to learn what kinds of people would give you money and what for, and remember the back doors of which food pantries or restaurants had kind and generous servers. The biggest problem was finding food and storing it for later. She deliberately made no friends of any kind—young or old, stable or wandering nuts. Anybody could turn you in or hurt you. Corner hookers were the nicest and the ones who warned her about dangers in their trade—guys who didn't pay, cops who did before arresting them, men who hurt them for fun. Rain said she didn't need reminding because once when some really old guy hurt her so bad she bled, her mother slapped him and screamed, "Get out!" then she douched her with a yellow powder. Men scared her, Rain confessed, and made her feel sick. She had been waiting on some steps at the Salvation Army truck stop when it began to rain. A lady on the truck might give her a coat or shoes this time like other times when she had slipped her food. That's when Evelyn and Steve came along, and when he touched her she thought of the men who came to her mother's house, so she had to run off, miss the food lady and hide.

Rain giggled on occasion as she described her homeless life, relishing her smarts, her escapes, while Bride fought against the danger of tears for anyone other than herself. Listening to this tough little girl who wasted no time on self-pity, she felt a companionship that was surprisingly free of envy. Like the closeness of schoolgirls.

Rain

She's gone, my black lady. That time I saw her stuck in the car her eyes scared me at first. Silky, my cat, has eyes like that. But it wasn't long before I began to like her a lot. She's so pretty. Sometimes I used to just look at her when she was sleeping. Today her car came back with a busted-up door of another color. Before she left she gave me a shaving brush. Steve has a beard and doesn't want it so I use it to brush my cat's fur. I feel sad now she's gone. I don't know who I can talk to. Evelyn is real good to me and so is Steve but they frown or look away if I say stuff about how it was in my mother's house or if I start to tell them how smart I was when I was thrown out. Anyway I don't want to kill them like I used to when I first got here. But then I wanted to kill everybody—until they brought me a kitten. She's a cat now and I tell her everything. My black lady listens to me tell how it was. Steve won't let me talk about it. Neither will Evelyn. They think I can read but I can't, well maybe a little—signs and stuff. Evelyn is trying to teach me. She calls it home-schooling. I call it home-drooling and home-fooling. We're a fake family—okay but fake. Evelyn is a good substi-

tute mother but I'd rather have a sister like my black lady. I
don't have a daddy, I mean I don't know who he is because
he didn't live in my mother's house but Steve is always here
unless he's doing some day work somewhere. My black lady
is nice but tough too. When we started walking back home
after I told her everything about my life before Evelyn and
Steve, a truck with big boys in it passed us. One of them
hollered "Hey, Rain. Who's your mammy?" My black lady
didn't turn around but I stuck out my tongue and thumbed
my nose at him. One of them was Regis, a boy I know
because he comes to our house sometimes with his father to
give us firewood or baskets of corn. The driver, an older boy,
turned the truck around so they could come after us. Regis
pointed a shotgun just like Steve's at us. My black lady saw
him and threw her arm in front of my face. The birdshot
messed up her hand and arm. We fell, both of us, her on
top of me. I saw Regis duck down as the truck gunned its
engine and shot off. What could I do but help her up and
hold on to her bloody arm as we hurried back to our house
as fast as her ankle would let her. Steve picked the tiny pel-
lets out of her hand and arm, saying he was going to warn
Regis's father. Evelyn washed the blood off my black lady's
skin and poured iodine all over her hand. My black lady
made a hurt face but she didn't cry. My heart was beating
fast because nobody had done that before. I mean Steve and
Evelyn took me in and all but nobody put their own self in

danger to save me. Save my life. But that's what my black lady did without even thinking about it.

She's gone now but who knows maybe I'll see her again sometime.

I miss my black lady.

PART III

Blood stained his knuckles and his fingers began to swell. The stranger he'd been beating wasn't moving anymore or groaning, but he knew he'd better walk away quickly before a student or campus guard thought he was the lawless one instead of the man lying on the grass. He'd left the beaten man's jeans open and his penis exposed just the way it was when he first saw him at the edge of the campus playground. Only a few faculty children were near the slide and one was on the swing. None apparently had noticed the man licking his lips and waving his little white gristle toward them. It was the lip licking that got to him— the tongue grazing the upper lip, the swallowing before its return to grazing. Obviously the sight of the children was as pleasurable to the man as touching them because just as obviously, in his warped mind, they were calling to him and he was answering their plump thighs and their tight little behinds, beckoning in panties or shorts as they climbed up to the slide or pumped air on the swing.

Booker's fist was in the man's mouth before thinking about it. A light spray of blood dappled his sweatshirt, and when the man lost consciousness, Booker grabbed his book bag off the ground and walked away—not too fast, but fast enough to cross the road, turn his shirt inside out and make it to class on time. He didn't make it, but there were a few others sneaking into the lecture hall when he arrived. The latecomers took seats in the last rows and plopped backpacks, briefcases or laptops on their desks. Only one of them took a notebook out. Booker preferred pencil on paper too, but his swollen fingers made writing difficult. So he listened a little, daydreamed a little and covered his mouth to hide his yawns.

The professor was going on and on about Adam Smith's wrongheadedness, as he did in almost every lecture, as though the history of economics had only one scholar worth trashing. What about Milton Friedman or that chameleon Karl Marx? Booker's obsession with Mammon was recent. Four years ago, as an undergraduate, he'd nibbled courses in several curricula, psychology, political science, humanities, and he'd taken multiple courses in African-American Studies, where the best professors were brilliant at description but could not answer to his satisfaction any question beginning with "Why." He suspected most of the real answers concerning slavery, lynching, forced labor, sharecropping, racism, Reconstruction, Jim Crow, prison labor, migration, civil rights and black revolution movements were all about money. Money withheld, money stolen, money as power, as war. Where was the lecture on how slavery alone catapulted the whole country from agriculture into the industrial age in two decades? White folks' hatred, their violence, was the gasoline that kept the profit motors running. So as a graduate student he turned to economics—its history, its theories—to learn how money shaped every single oppression in the world and created all the empires, nations, colonies with God and His enemies employed to reap, then veil, the riches. He habitually contrasted the beaten, penniless, half-naked King of the Jews screaming betrayal on a cross with the bejeweled, glamorously dressed pope whispering homilies above the Vatican's vault. *The Cross and the Vault* by Booker Starbern. That would be the title of his book.

Unimpressed by the lecture, he let his thoughts slide toward the man lying exposed near the playground. Bald. Normal-looking. Probably an otherwise nice man—they always were. The "nicest man in the world," the neighbors always said. "He wouldn't hurt a fly." Where did that cliché come from? Why not hurt a fly? Did it mean he was too tender to take the life of a disease-carrying insect but could happily ax the life of a child?

Booker had been raised in a large, tight family with no television in sight. As a freshman in college he lived surrounded by a television/Internet world where both the methods of mass communication and the substance of mass communication seemed to him loaded with entertainment but mostly free of insight or knowledge. The weather channels were the only informative sources but they were off-base and hysterical most of the time. And the video games—mesmerizing in pointlessness. Having grown up in a book-reading family with only radio and newspapers for day-to-day information and vinyl records for entertainment, he had to fake his classmates' enthusiasm for the screen sounds of games blasting from every dorm room, lounge and student-friendly bar. He knew he was way, way out of the loop—a Luddite incapable of sharing the exciting world of tech, and it had embarrassed him as a freshman. He had been shaped by talk in the flesh and text on paper. Every Saturday morning, first thing before breakfast, his parents held conferences with their children requiring them to answer two questions put to each of them: 1. What have you learned that is true (and how do you know)? 2. What problem do you have? Over the years answers to the first question ranged from "Worms can't fly," "Ice burns," "There are only three counties in this state," to "The pawn is mightier than the queen." Topics relevant to the second question might be "A girl slapped me," "My acne is back," "Algebra," "The conjugation of Latin verbs." Questions about personal problems prompted solutions from anyone at the table, and after they were solved or left pending, the children were sent to bathe and dress—the older ones helping the younger. Booker loved those Saturday morning conferences rewarded by the highlight of the weekend—his mother's huge breakfast feasts. Banquets, really. Hot biscuits, short and flaky; grits, snow-white and tongue-burning hot; eggs beaten into pale saffron creaminess; sizzling sausage patties, sliced tomatoes, strawberry jam, freshly squeezed orange juice, cold milk in Mason jars. Some food she stored up for those weekend feasts because during the rest of the week they ate frugally: oatmeal, in-season fruit, rice, dried beans and whatever green leaf was available: kale, spinach, cabbage, collards, mustard or turnip greens. Those weekend breakfast menus were deliberately sumptuous because they followed days of scarcity.

Only during the long months when no one knew where Adam was did the family conferences and sumptuous breakfasts stop. During those months quiet ticked through the house like a time bomb that would often explode into quarrels, silly and pointlessly mean.

"Ma, he's looking at me!"

"Stop looking at her."

"He's looking back!"

"Stop looking back."

"Ma!"

When the police responded to their plea for help in searching for Adam, they immediately searched the Starberns' house—as though the anxious parents might be at fault. They checked to see if the father had a police record. He didn't. "We'll get back to you," they said. Then they dropped it. Another little black boy gone. So?

Booker's father refused to play even one of his beloved ragtime, old-time, jazzy records, some of which Booker could do without but not Satchmo. It was one thing to lose a brother—that broke his heart—but a world without Louis Armstrong's trumpet crushed it.

Then at the beginning of spring, when lawn trees started preening, Adam was found. In a culvert.

Booker went with his father to identify the remains. Filthy, rat-gnawed, with a single open eye socket. The maggots, overfed and bursting with glee, had gone home leaving fastidiously clean bones under the strips of his mud-caked yellow T-shirt. The corpse wore no pants or shoes. Booker's mother could not go there. She refused to have etched in her brain anything other than her image of her firstborn's young, outrageous beauty.

The closed-coffin funeral seemed cheap and lonely to Booker in spite of the preacher's loud eloquence, the crowds of neighbors attending, the dish after dish of carefully cooked food delivered to their kitchen. The very excess made him lonelier. It was as though his older brother, close as a twin, was being buried again, suffocating under song, sermon, tears, crowds and flowers. He wanted to redirect the mourning—make it private, special and, most of all, his alone. Adam was the brother he worshipped, two years older and sweet as cane. A flawless replacement for the brother he'd curled up with in the womb. A brother, he was told, who didn't take a single living breath. Booker was three when they let him know he was a twin to the one who did not survive birth, but somehow he'd always known it—felt the warm void walking by his side, or waiting on the porch steps while he played in the yard. A presence that shared the quilt under which Booker slept. As he grew older the shape of the void faded, transferred itself into a kind of inner companion, one whose reactions and instincts he trusted. When he started first grade and walked to school every day with Adam the replacement was complete. So, following Adam's murder, Booker had no companion. Both were dead.

The last time Booker saw Adam he was skateboarding down the sidewalk in twilight, his yellow T-shirt fluorescent under the Northern Ash trees. It was early September and nothing anywhere had begun to die. Maple leaves behaved as though their green was immortal. Ash trees were still climbing toward a cloudless sky. The sun began turning aggressively alive in the process of setting. Down the sidewalk between hedges and towering trees Adam floated, a spot of gold moving down a shadowy tunnel toward the mouth of a living sun.

Adam was more than brother to Booker, more than the

"A" of parents who'd named their children alphabetically. He was the one who knew what Booker was thinking, feeling, whose humor was both raucous and instructive but never cruel, the smartest one who loved each of his siblings but especially Booker.

Unable to forget that final glow of yellow tunneling down the street, Booker placed a single yellow rose on the coffin lid and another, later, graveside. Family members came long distances to bury the dead and comfort the Starberns. Among them was Mr. Drew, his mother's father. He was the successful one, the grandfather openly hostile to everybody not as rich as he was, the one even his daughter called not "Daddy" or "Papa" but "Mr. Drew." Yet the old man, who had made his money as an unforgiving slumlord, minded what was left of his manners and did not show the contempt he felt for this struggling family.

After the funeral the house returned tentatively to its routine, with the encouraging sounds of Louis, Ella, Sidney Bechet, Jelly Roll, King Oliver and Bunk Johnson floating from the record player in the background. And the conferences and breakfast feasts returned, with Booker and his siblings, Carole, Donovan, Ellie, Favor and Goodman, all trying to think up interesting answers to the routine questions. In time the whole family perked up like *Sesame Street* puppets, hoping that cheer, if worked at hard enough, could sugar the living and quiet the dead. Booker thought their joking strained and their made-up problems both misguided and insulting. During the funeral and for a few days after, a visiting relative, an aunt they called Queen, was the exception to what Booker thought was mindless rote. She had a last name that no one remembered since she was rumored to have had many husbands—one a Mexican, then two white men, four black men, one Asian, but in a sequence no one recalled. Heavy-set with fire-red hair, she surprised the grieving family by traveling all the way from California to attend Adam's funeral. She alone sensed her nephew's anger-mixed sorrow and pulled him aside.

"Don't let him go," she said. "Not until he's ready. Meantime, hang on to him tooth and claw. Adam will let you know when it's time."

She comforted him, strengthened him and validated the unfairness of the censure he was feeling from his family.

Wary of another crisis that might eliminate the soul-stretching music his father played, which Booker counted on to oil and straighten his tangled feelings, he asked his father if he could take trumpet lessons. Sure, said Mr. Starbern, provided his son earned half the teacher's fee. Booker nagged his neighbors for chores and earned enough to skip the Saturday conferences for trumpet lessons that dampened his budding intolerance for his siblings. How could they pretend it was over? How could they forget and just go on? Who and where was the murderer?

His trumpet teacher, already slightly drunk early in the morning, was nevertheless an excellent musician and an even better instructor.

"You got the lungs, the fingers, now you need the lip. When you get all three together you can forget about them and let the music out."

Which, with persistence, he did.

Six years later when Booker was fourteen and a faintly accomplished trumpet player, the nicest man in the world was caught, tried and convicted of SSS, the sexually stimulated slaughter of six boys, each of whose names, including Adam's, was tattooed across the shoulders of the nicest man in the world. Boise. Lenny. Adam. Matthew. Kevin. Roland. Clearly an equal-opportunity killer, his victims seemed to be representative of the *We Are the World* video. The tattoo artist said he thought they were the names of his client's children, not those of other people.

The nicest man in the world was an easygoing, retired auto mechanic who solicited home repairs. He was especially helpful with old refrigerators—the Philcos and GE's built in the fifties to last, and ancient gas stoves and furnaces. "Dirt," he used to say. "Most machinery died because it was never cleaned." Everyone who had hired him recalled that advice. Another feature some remembered was his smile, how welcoming, attractive, even. Otherwise he was fastidious, capable and, well, nice. The single other thing people remembered most about him was that he always traveled with a cute little dog in his van, a terrier he called "Boy." The police withheld what details they could but the families of the murdered boys could not be stopped or silenced. Nightmares about what might have been done to their children did not outweigh the facts. Six years of grief and unanswered questions coalesced around their recollections of time spent in the morgue, heaving, weeping, stone-faced or on their backs in helpless faints.

There was not much left of Adam when he was found, but the details of the more recent abductions were Gothic. Apparently the children were kept bound while molested, tortured and there were amputations. The nicest man in the world must have used his small white terrier as a lure. A central witness, an elderly widow, remembered that she had seen a child in the passenger side of his van laughing and holding a little dog up to his face. Later, after seeing the missing-child posters displayed in store windows, on telephone poles and trees, she thought she recognized a face as that of the laughing boy. She called the police. Of course they knew the van. It advertised in red and blue letters its promise: PROBLEM? SOLVED! WM. V. HUMBOLDT. HOME REPAIR. When Mr. Humboldt's house was searched a dirty mattress sporting dried blood was found in the basement along with an elaborately decorated candy tin that held carefully wrapped pieces of dry flesh, which, on not very close inspection, turned out to be small penises.

Public demands and cries for vengeance disguised as

justice were rampant and harrowing. Signs, rallies in front of the courthouse, editorials—all seemed unassuageable by anything less than the culprit's beheading. Booker joined the chorus but was not impressed by so facile a solution. What he wanted was not the man's death; he wanted his life, and spent time inventing scenarios involving pain and despair without end. Wasn't there a tribe in Africa that lashed the dead body to the back of the one who had murdered it? That would certainly be justice—to carry the rotting corpse around as a physical burden as well as public shame and damnation. The rage, the public clamor upon the conviction of the nicest man in the world, shook him almost as much as Adam's death. The trial itself was not long but the preliminaries seemed eternal to Booker. Throughout the days of newspaper headlines, talk radio and neighborhood gossip he struggled to find some way to freeze and individualize his feelings, to separate them from the sorrow and frenzied anger of other families. Adam's calamity, he thought, was not public fare to be confined to one line in a newspaper's list of the six victims. It was private, belonging only to the two brothers. Two years later, a satisfactory and calming solution came to him. Reenacting the gesture he'd made at Adam's funeral, he had a small rose tattooed on his left shoulder. Was this the same chair the predator sat in, the same needle used on his paste-white skin? He didn't ask. The tattoo artist didn't have the dazzling yellow of Booker's memory, so they settled for an orangish kind of red.

Being accepted into college offered relief as well as distraction and he soon became enchanted with campus life— not the classes, not the professors, but his lively, know-it-all classmates, an enchantment that did not wane for two years. All he did from freshman year through sophomore was react—sneer, laugh, dismiss, find fault, demean—a young man's version of critical thinking. He and his dorm mates ranked girls according to men's magazines and porn videos, ranked one another according to characters in action movies they had seen. The clever ones breezed through classes; the geniuses dropped out. It was as a junior that his mild cynicism morphed into depression. The views of his classmates began to both bore and bother him, not only because they were predictable but also because they blocked serious inquiry. Unlike his effort to perfect "Wild Cat Blues" on his trumpet, no new or creative thinking was required in undergraduate society and none penetrated the blessed fog of young transgression. Student agitation about the war in Iraq that once roiled the campus had quieted. Now sarcasm fluttered its triumphant flag and giggles became its oath; now the docile manipulation of professors became routine. So Booker replayed those questions posed by his parents during those Saturday conferences on Decatur Street: 1. What have you learned that is true (and how do you know)? 2. What problem do you have?

1. So far nothing. 2. Despair.

So, hoping to learn something of value and perhaps find an accommodating place for despair, he applied to graduate school. There he focused on tracking wealth from barter to bombs. To him it was a riveting intellectual journey that policed his anger, caged it and explained everything about racism, poverty and war. The political world was anathema; its activists, both retro and progressive, seemed wrongheaded and dreamy. The revolutionaries, armed or peaceful, had no notion of what should happen after they "won." Who would rule? The "people"? Please. What did that mean? The best outcome would be to introduce a new idea into the population that perhaps a politician would act on. The rest was theater seeking an audience. Wealth alone explained humanity's evil, and he was determined to live without deference to it. He knew exactly the subjects and themes of the articles and books he would write and kept notes on his research. Other than the scholarship in his field he read a little poetry and some journals. No novels—great or lesser. He liked certain poems because they paralleled music, journals because the essays bled politics into culture. It was during his graduate school days that he began to write something other than outlines for future essays. He began trying to shape unpunctuated sentences into musical language that expressed his questions about or results of his thinking. Most of these he trashed; a few he kept.

Assured finally of his master's degree, Booker traveled home alone for the celebratory dinner his mother had arranged. He thought about asking Felicity, his on-again, off-again girlfriend, to accompany him, but decided against it. He didn't want an outsider judging his family. That was his job.

Everything was smooth and almost cheerful at the family gathering until he went upstairs to his old bedroom, the one he once shared with Adam. Looking for what, he was not sure. The room was not simply different; it was antagonistic—a double bed instead of his and Adam's twin set, white transparent curtains instead of shades, a cutesy rug under a tiny desk. Worst of all, the closet that used to be jammed with their playthings—bats, basketballs, board games—now held his sister Carole's girl clothes. But resentment choked him when he discovered that his old skateboard, identical to the one that disappeared along with Adam, was gone. Weak with sadness, Booker went back downstairs. But when he saw his sister, his pallid weakness changed into its blazing twin—fury. He picked a quarrel with Carole; she argued back. Their fight escalated and disturbed the whole family until Mr. Starbern shut it down.

"Stop it, Booker! You not the only one grieving. Folks

mourn in different ways." His father's voice was like the steel of a knife's edge.

"Yeah, sure." Booker's tone was hostile, laced with contempt.

"You acting like you the only one in this family who loved him. Adam wouldn't want that," said his father.

"You don't know what he'd want." Booker successfully fought back tears.

Mr. Starbern rose from the couch. "Well, I do know what I want. I want you civil in this house or out of it."

"Oh, no," Mrs. Starbern whispered. "Don't say that."

Father and son stared at each other, their eyes locking in military aggression. Mr. Starbern won the battle and Booker left the house, closing the door firmly behind him.

It was fitting, perhaps, that after leaving the only home he had ever known he would step out into a downpour. Rain forced him to raise his collar and duck his head like an intruder thankful for the night. Shoulders high, eyes squinting, he moved down Decatur Street in a mood the rainstorm complemented. Before his quarrel with Carole he'd tried to persuade his parents to think of some sort of memorial for Adam—a modest scholarship in his name, for example. His mother warmed to the idea, but his father frowned and was decidedly against it.

"We can't waste money like that and we can't waste time raising it," he said. "Besides, the people who admired and remember Adam don't need to be reminded."

Booker was already feeling a poisonous vein of disapproval not only from Carole, but his younger siblings as well. To Favor and Goodman it seemed Booker wanted a statue of a brother who died when they were babies. What Booker understood as family loyalty, the others saw as manipulation—as trying to control them—outfathering their father. Just because he had two college degrees he thought he could tell everybody what to do. They rolled their eyes at his arrogance.

When he visited his and Adam's old bedroom, the thread of disapproval he'd felt during his proposal of a memorial became a rope, as he saw the savage absence not only of Adam but of himself. So when he shut the door on his family and stepped out into the rain it was an already belated act.

Felicity said, "Okay, sure," when Booker asked if he could bunk at her place for a while. He was grateful for her quick response since he had no address of his own once he cleared out of the graduate dorm. On the bus back to campus reading the back issue of *Daedalus* he'd brought along distracted him from currying his disappointment with his family. But it surfaced powerfully when he got back to the dorm and began to throw the remnants of his college life into boxes—texts, running shoes, shapeless clothes, notebooks, journals—all except his loved trumpet. When he stopped wallowing in the self-pity of being outrageously misunderstood, he called his girlfriend. Felicity was a substitute teacher and their relationship had lasted two years primarily because there were sustained blocks of time when they didn't see each other. Her call-ups, based as they were on the sudden illness of a permanent teacher, were irregular and often to distant districts. So he felt comfortable asking whether he could move in for a bit since both knew it was about convenience and had nothing to do with commitment. It was summer, and since Felicity would probably have no requests for substituting, they could enjoy each other's company without deadlines: go to movies, eat out, run trails—whatever they felt like.

One evening Booker took Felicity to Pier 2, a run-down dinner-and-dancing club that boasted a live combo. Over the shrimp and rice Booker thought, as he often did, that the quartet on the little stage needed brass. Virtually all popular music was saturated with strings: guitars, basses and piano keys aided by percussion. Other than the big-star musicians like the E Street Band, or Wynton Marsalis's orchestra, groups seldom featured, in backup or solo, a sax, clarinet, trombone or trumpet, and he felt the void intensely. So this evening at the break he went backstage to the narrow dressing room full of weed smoke and laughing musicians to ask if he could join their group sometime. Not wanting to cut their earnings with another player, especially one they didn't know, they dismissed him quickly.

"Go to hell, man."

"Who let you back here?"

"Well you could at least hear me," he pleaded. "I play trumpet and you could do with a horn."

The guitarists rolled their eyes, but the drummer said, "Bring it to the Friday set. That's when it won't matter if you screw up."

He didn't mention his future audition to Felicity. She couldn't be less interested in his trumpet playing.

Booker did as the drummer suggested, trying out before them in the dressing room with as close as he could come to a Louis Armstrong solo. The drummer nodded, the piano player smiled and the two guitarists had no objection. From then on during the summer Booker joined the group calling itself The Big Boys on Fridays, when the place was so crowded the drinkers and diners paid no attention to the music.

When in September The Big Boys broke up—the drummer moved away; the piano player got a bigger, better gig—Booker and the guitarists, Michael and Freeman Chase, began to play on streets dappled with homeless veterans with cold fury in their eyes. Their anger was not dampened by the fact that they got more generous offerings by being surrounded by music. It was the sweetest season of Booker's life but it didn't last. By the end of summer the relationship with Felicity had frayed beyond any stitched-up remedy. They had enjoyed being roommate lovers the whole summer before each began to annoy the other with habits they had not previously paid close attention to. Felicity complained about his loud trumpet practice and his refusal to party every single night with her friends. He hated her cigarette smoke, her choices of take-out food, music and wine. In addition to insisting on constant visits from members of her family, she was nosy, forever prying into his life. Most of all he found her to be insufferably opinionated. In fact Felicity found him as unpleasant and annoying as he found her. She believed she might lose her sanity if she had to listen one more time to Donald Byrd or Freddie Hubbard or Blue Mitchell or any of his other favorite musicians. She began to regard him as a misogynist loser. Nevertheless they might have stayed together, in spite of the mutual hostility that was growing like mold between them, except for one event: Booker's arrest and the night he spent in a holding cell.

He had passed a couple, parked near an empty lot, taking turns sucking on a crack pipe. The sight was of no interest to him until he noticed a child, maybe two years old, screaming and crying while standing in the backseat of the crackheads' Toyota. He walked over to the car, yanked open the door, dragged the man out, smashed his face and kicked away the pipe that had fallen to the ground. Then the woman jumped out and ran to help her partner. The three-person fight was more hilarious than lethal, but it was long enough and loud enough to get the attention first of shoppers, then the police. All three were arrested and the little screaming girl given to childcare services.

Felicity had to pay the fine. The judge was lenient with Booker because the crackhead parents disgusted him as much as they did Booker. He arraigned the couple and issued a disturbing-the-peace ticket for Booker. The entire incident enraged Felicity who wondered aloud why he meddled in things that didn't concern him.

"Who do you think you are? Batman?"

Booker fingered his right molar to see if it was loose or broken. The female had had more strength than the man, who swung wildly but never got in a hit. It was her knuckles that connected with his jaw.

"There was a little kid in that car. A baby!" he said.

"It wasn't your kid and it wasn't your business," shouted Felicity.

A mite loose, decided Booker, but he would see a dentist anyway.

On the bus home each knew it was over without saying so. Felicity continued nagging for an hour or so after they arrived at her apartment, but up against Booker's leaden silence, she quit and took a shower. He didn't join her, as had been their practice.

Booker's work history was thin—one embarrassing and disaster-ridden semester teaching music in a junior high school, the only public school teaching he could do since he had no certificate, and he was cut from the few music auditions he signed up for. His trumpet talent was adequate but not exceptional.

His luck changed at the precise moment it needed to when Carole tracked him down to forward a letter addressed to him from a law firm. Mr. Drew had died and to everyone's surprise he had included his grandchildren— but not his own children—in his will. Booker was to share the old man's constantly-bragged-about fortune with his siblings. He refused to think about the greed and criminality that produced his grandfather's fortune. He told himself the slumlord money had been cleansed by death. Not bad. Now he could rent his own place, a quiet room in a quiet neighborhood, and continue playing either on the street or in more little rundown clubs. Having access to no studio, the men played on corners. Not for money, which was pitiful enough, but to practice and experiment with one another in public before a nonpaying, therefore uncritical, undemanding audience.

Then came a day that changed him and his music.

Simply dumbstruck by her beauty Booker stared openmouthed at a young blue-black woman standing at the curb laughing. Her clothes were white, her hair like a million black butterflies asleep on her head. She was talking to another woman—chalk white with blond dreadlocks. A limousine negotiated the curb and both waited for the driver to open the door for them. Although it made him sad to see the limo pull away, Booker smiled and smiled as he walked on to the train entrance, where he played with the two guitarists. Neither one was there, not Michael or Chase, and it was only then that he noticed the rain—soft, steady. The sun still blazed so the raindrops falling from a baby-blue sky were like crystal breaking into specks of light on the pavement. He decided to play his trumpet alone in the rain anyway, knowing that no pedestrians would stop to listen; rather, they closed umbrellas as they rushed down the stairs to the trains. Still in thrall to the sheer beauty of the girl he had seen, he put the trumpet to his lips. What emerged was music he had never played before. Low, muted notes held long, too long, as the strains floated through drops of rain.

Booker had no words to describe his feelings. What he did know was that the rain-soaked air smelled like lilac when he played while remembering her. Streets with litter at their curbs appeared interesting, not filthy; bodegas, beauty shops, diners, thrift stores leaning against one another looked homey, downright friendly. Each time he imagined her eyes glittering toward him or her lips open in an inviting, reckless smile, he felt not just a swell of desire but also the disintegration of the haunt and gloom in which for years Adam's death had clouded him. When he stepped through that cloud and became as emotionally content as he had been before Adam skated into the sunset—there she was. A midnight Galatea always and already alive.

A few weeks after that first sighting of her waiting for a limousine, there she was again, standing in line at the stadium where the Black Gauchos were performing—a hot band, new, upcoming, playing a blend of Brazilian and New Orleans jazz, one show only. The line was long, loud and jittery but when the doors opened to the crush he managed first to slip four bodies behind her and then, when the crowd found bench seats, he was able to stand right at her back.

In music-powered air, with body rules broken and sexual benevolence thick as cream, circling her waist with his arms seemed more than a natural gesture; it was an inevitable one. And together they danced and danced. When the music stopped, his Galatea turned to face him and surrender to him the reckless smile he'd always imagined.

"Bride," she said when he asked her name.

God damn, he whispered.

Their lovemaking from the very beginning was serene, artful and long-lasting, so necessary to Booker that he deliberately withheld for nights in a row to make the return to her

bed brand-new. Their relationship was flawless. He especially liked her lack of interest in his personal life. Unlike
with Felicity there was no probing. Bride was knock-down
beautiful, easy, had something to do every day and didn't
need his presence every minute. Her self-love was consistent
with her cosmetic company milieu and mirrored his obsession with her. So if she rattled on about coworkers, products
and markets, he watched her mesmerizing eyes that were so
deeply expressive they said much more than mere language
could. Speaking-eyes, he thought, accompanied by the
music of her voice. Every feature—the ledge of her cheek-
bones, her invitational mouth, her nose, forehead, chin as
well as those eyes—was more exquisite, more aesthetically
pleasing because of her obsidian-midnight skin. Whether
he was lying under her body, hovering above it or holding
her in his arms, her blackness thrilled him. Then he was
certain that he not only held the night, he owned it, and
if the night he held in his arms was not enough, he could
always see starlight in her eyes. Her innocent, oblivious sense
of humor delighted him. When she, who wore no makeup
and worked in a business all about cosmetics, asked him to
help her choose the most winning shade of lip gloss, he laughed
out loud. Her insistence on white-only clothes amused him.
Unwilling to share her with the public he was seldom in
the mood for clubbing. Yet dancing with her in down-lit
uncool clubrooms to tapes of Michael Jackson's soprano

or James Brown's shouts was irresistible. Pressing close to her in crowded rap bars bewitched them both. He refused her nothing except accompanying her on shopping sprees.

Once in a while she dropped the hip, thrillingly successful corporate woman façade of complete control and confessed some flaw or painful memory of childhood. And he, knowing all about how childhood cuts festered and never scabbed over, comforted her while hiding the rage he felt at the idea of anyone hurting her.

Bride's complicated relationship with her mother and repellent father meant that, like him, she was free of family ties. It was just the two of them, and with the exception of her obnoxious pseudo-friend Brooklyn there were fewer and fewer interruptions from her colleagues. He still played with Chase and Michael on weekends, some afternoons, but there were glorious mornings of sun at the shore, cool evenings holding hands in the park in anticipation of the sexual choreography they would perform in every nook of her apartment. Sober as priests, creative as devils, they invented sex. So they believed.

When Bride was at her office, Booker relished the solitude for trumpet practice, scribbling notes to mail to his favorite aunt, Queen, and since there were no books in Bride's apartment—just fashion and gossip magazines— he visited the library often to read or reread books he had ignored or misunderstood while at university. *The Name of the Rose,* for one, and *Remembering Slavery,* a collection that so moved him he composed some mediocre, sentimental music to commemorate the narratives. He read Twain, enjoying the cruelty of his humor. He read Walter Benjamin, impressed by the beauty of the translation, he read Frederick Douglass's autobiography again, relishing for the first time the eloquence that both hid and displayed his hatred. He read Herman Melville, and let Pip break his heart, reminding him of Adam alone, abandoned, swallowed by waves of casual evil.

Six months into the bliss of edible sex, free-style music, challenging books and the company of an easy undemanding Bride, the fairy-tale castle collapsed into the mud and sand on which its vanity was built. And Booker ran away.

PART IV

Brooklyn

Nothing. A call to our CO asking for more extended leave. Rehab. Emotional rehab—whatever. But nothing about where she's headed or why until today. A note scribbled on a piece of yellow lined tablet paper. Christ. I didn't have to read it to know what it said. "Sorry I ran away. I had to. Except for you everything was falling apart blah, blah, blah . . ."

Beautiful dumb bitch. Nothing about where she's going or how long she'd be gone. One thing I know for sure she's tracking that guy. I can read her mind like a headline crawling across the bottom of a TV screen. It's a gift I've had since I was a little kid. Like when the landlady stole the money lying on our dining room table and said we were behind in the rent. Or when my uncle started thinking of putting his fingers between my legs again, even before he knew himself what he was planning to do. I hid or ran or screamed with a fake stomachache so my mother would wake from her drunken nap to tend to me. Believe it. I've always sensed what people want and how to please them. Or not. Only once did I misread—with Bride's loverman.

I ran away, too, Bride, but I was fourteen and there was nobody but me to take care of me so I invented myself, toughened myself. I thought you did too except when it came to boyfriends. I knew right away that the last one—a conman if ever I saw one—would turn you into the scared little girl you used to be. One fight with a crazy felon and you surrendered, stupid enough to quit the best job in the world.

I started out sweeping a hairdresser's shop then waitressing until I got the drugstore job. Long before Sylvia, Inc., I fought like the devil for each job I ever got and let nothing, nothing stop me.

But for you it's "Wah, wah, I had to run . . ." Where to? In some place where there is no real stationery or even a postcard?

Bride, please.

A city girl is quickly weary of the cardboard boredom of tiny rural towns. Whatever the weather, iron-bright sunshine or piercing rain, the impression of worn boxes hiding shiftless residents seems to sap the most attentive gaze. It's one thing for onetime hippies to live their anticapitalist ideals near the edge of a seldom-traveled country road. Evelyn and Steve had lived exciting lives of risk and purpose in their adventurous pasts. But what about regular plain folks who were born in these places and never left? Bride wasn't feeling superior to the line of tiny, melancholy houses and mobile homes on each side of the road, just puzzled. What would make Booker choose this place? And who the hell is Q. Olive?

She had driven one hundred and seventy miles on and off dirt roads some of which must have been created originally by moccasin-shod feet and wolf packs. Truckers could navigate them but a Jaguar repaired with another model's door had serious trouble. Bride drove carefully, peering ahead for obstacles, alive or not. By the time she saw the sign nailed to the trunk of a pine tree, her exhaustion quieted a growing alarm. Although there were no more physical disappearances, she was disturbed by the fact that she'd had no menstrual period for at least two, maybe three, months. Flat-chested and without underarm or pubic hair, pierced ears and stable weight, she tried and failed to forget what she believed was her crazed transformation back into a scared little black girl.

Whiskey, it turned out, was half a dozen or so houses on both sides of a gravel road that led to a stretch of trailers and mobile homes. Parallel to the road beyond a stretch of sorrowful-looking trees ran a deep but narrow stream. The houses had no addresses but some mobile homes had names painted on sturdy mailboxes. Under eyes suspicious of strange cars and stranger visitors, Bride cruised slowly until she saw QUEEN OLIVE printed on a mailbox in front of a pale-yellow mobile home. She parked, got out and was walking toward the door when she smelled gasoline and fire that seemed to be coming from behind the home. When she crept toward the backyard she saw a heavyset red-headed woman sprinkling gasoline on a metal bedspring, carefully noting where flames needed to be fed.

Bride hurried back to her car and waited. Two children came along, attracted, perhaps, by the fancy automobile, but distracted by the woman at the wheel. Both stared at her for what seemed like minutes in unblinking wonder. Bride ignored the dumbstruck children. She knew well what it was to walk into a room and see the exchange of looks between white strangers. The looks were dismissible because, most often, the gasps her blackness provoked were invariably followed by the envy her beauty produced. Although, with Jeri's help, she had capitalized on her dark skin, stressing it, glamorizing it, she recalled an exchange she once had with Booker. Complaining about her mother, she told him that Sweetness hated her for her black skin.

"It's just a color," Booker had said. "A genetic trait—not a flaw, not a curse, not a blessing nor a sin."

"But," she countered, "other people think racial—"

Booker cut her off. "Scientifically there's no such thing as race, Bride, so racism without race is a choice. Taught, of course, by those who need it, but still a choice. Folks who practice it would be nothing without it."

His words were rational and, at the time, soothing but had little to do with day-to-day experience—like sitting in a car under the stunned gaze of little white children who couldn't be more fascinated if they were at a museum of dinosaurs. Nevertheless, she flat out refused to be derailed from her mission simply because she was outside the comfort zone of paved streets, tight lawns surrounded by racially diverse people who might not help but would not harm her. Determined to discover what she was made of—cotton or steel—there could be no retreat, no turning back.

Half an hour passed; the children were gone and a nickel-plated sun at the top of the sky warmed the car's interior. Taking a deep breath, Bride walked to the yellow door and knocked. When the female arsonist appeared she said, "Hello. Excuse me. I'm looking for Booker Starbern. This is the address I have for him."

"That figures," said the woman. "I get a lot of his mail—magazines, catalogs, stuff he writes himself."

"Is he here?" Bride was dazzled by the woman's earrings, golden discs the size of clamshells.

"Uh-uh." The woman shook her head while boring into Bride's eyes. "He's nearby, though."

"He is? Well how far is nearby?" Relieved that Q. Olive was not a young rival, Bride sighed and asked directions.

"You can walk it, but come on in. Booker ain't going nowhere. He's laid up—broke his arm. Come on in. You look like something a raccoon found and refused to eat."

Bride swallowed. For the past three years she'd only been told how exotic, how gorgeous she was—everywhere, from almost everybody—stunning, dreamy, hot, wow! Now this old woman with woolly red hair and judging eyes had deleted an entire vocabulary of compliments in one stroke. Once again she was the ugly, too-black little girl in her mother's house.

Queen curled her finger. "Get in here, girl. You need feeding."

"Look, Miss Olive—"

"Just Queen, honey. And it's Ol-li-vay. Step on in here. I don't get much company and I know hungry when I see it."

Well, that's true, thought Bride. Her anxiety during

the long trip had masked her stomach-yelling hunger. She obeyed Queen and was pleasantly surprised at the room's orderliness, comfort and charm. She had wondered for a second if she was being seduced into a witch's den. Obviously Queen sewed, knitted, crocheted and made lace. Curtains, slipcovers, cushions, embroidered napkins were elegantly handmade. A quilt on the headboard of an empty bed, whose springs were apparently cooling outside, was pieced in soft colors and, like everything else, cleverly mismatched. Small antiques such as picture frames and side tables were oddly placed. One whole wall was covered with photographs of children. A pot simmered on the two-burner stove. Queen, unaccustomed to being rebuffed, placed two porcelain bowls on linen mats along with matching napkins and silver soup spoons with filigreed handles.

Bride sat down at a narrow table on a chair with a decorative seat cushion and watched Queen ladle thick soup into their bowls. Pieces of chicken floated among peas, potatoes, corn kernels, tomato, celery, green peppers, spinach and a scattering of pasta shells. Bride couldn't identify the strong seasonings—curry? Cardamom? Garlic? Cayenne? Black pepper and red? But the result was manna. Queen added a basket of warm flat bread, joined her guest and blessed the food. Neither spoke for long minutes of eating. Finally, Bride looked up from her bowl, wiped her lips, sighed and asked her hostess, "Why were you burning your bedsprings? I saw you back there."

"Bedbugs," answered Queen. "Every year I burn them out before the eggs get started."

"Oh. I never heard of that." Then, feeling more comfortable with the woman, asked, "What kind of stuff did Booker send you? You said he sent some writings."

"Uh-huh. He did. Every now and then."

"What were they about?"

"Beats me. I'll show you some, if you like. Say, why you looking for Booker? He owe you money? You sure can't be his woman. You sound like you don't know him too good."

"I don't, but I thought I did." She didn't say so, but it suddenly occurred to her that good sex was not knowledge. It was barely information.

Bride touched the napkin to her lips again. "We were living together, then he dumped me. Just like that." Bride snapped her fingers. "He left me without a word."

Queen chuckled. "Oh he's a leaver, all right. Left his own family. All except me."

"He did? Why?" Bride didn't like being classified with Booker's family, but the news surprised her.

"His older brother was murdered when they was kids and he didn't approve of his folks' response."

"Awww," Bride murmured. "That's sad." She made the acceptable sound of sympathy but was shocked to learn she knew nothing about it.

"More than sad. Almost ruined the family."

"What did they do that made him leave?"

"They moved on. Started to live life like it was life. He wanted them to establish a memorial, a foundation or something in his brother's name. They weren't interested. At all. I have to take some responsibility for the breakup. I told him to keep his brother close, mourn him as long as he needed to. I didn't count on what he took away from what I said. Anyhow, Adam's death became his own life. I think it's his only life." Queen glanced at Bride's empty bowl. "More?"

"No thanks, but it was delicious. I don't remember eating anything that good."

Queen smiled. "It's my United Nations recipe from the food of all my husbands' hometowns. Seven, from Delhi to Dakar, from Texas to Australia, and a few in between." She was laughing, her shoulders rocking. "So many men and all of them the same where it counts."

"Where does it count?"

"Ownership."

All those husbands and still all alone, thought Bride. "Don't you have any kids?" Obviously she did; their photographs were everywhere.

"Lots. Two live with their fathers and their new wives; two in the military—one a marine, one in the air force; another one, my last, a daughter, is in medical school. She's my dream child. The next to last is filthy rich somewhere in New York City. Most of them send me money so they don't have to come see me. But I see them." She waved to the photographs gazing out from exquisite frames. "And I know how and what they think. Booker always stayed in touch with me, though. Here, I'll show you how and what he thinks." Queen moved to a cabinet where sewing materials were neatly hanging or stacked. From its floor she lifted an old-fashioned breadbox. After sorting through its contents, she removed a thin sheaf of papers clipped together and handed it to her guest.

What lovely handwriting, thought Bride, suddenly realizing that she'd never seen anything Booker wrote—not even his name. There were seven sheets. One for each month they were together—plus one more. She read the first page slowly, her forefinger tracing the lines, for there was little or no punctuation.

Hey girl what's inside your curly head besides dark
rooms with dark men dancing too close to comfort
the mouth hungry for more of what it is sure is there
somewhere out there just waiting for a tongue and some
breath to stroke teeth that bite the night and swallow
whole the world denied you so get rid of those smokey
dreams and lie on the beach in my arms while i cover
you with white sands from shores you have never seen
lapped by waters so crystal and blue they make you
shed tears of bliss and let you know that you do belong

finally to the planet you were born on and can now join
the out-there world in the deep peace of a cello.

Bride read the words twice, understanding little if anything. It was the second page that made her uncomfortable.

Her imagination is impeccable the way it cuts and
scrapes the bone never touching the marrow where
that dirty feeling is thrumming like a fiddle for fear its
strings will break and screech the loss of its tune since
for her permanent ignorance is so much better than the
quick of life.

Queen, having finished washing the dishes, offered her
guest a drink of whiskey. Bride declined.

Reading the third page, she thought she remembered a
conversation she'd had with Booker that could have provoked what he wrote, the one in which she described the
landlord and details of her childhood.

You accepted like a beast of burden the whip of a
stranger's curse and the mindless menace it holds along
with the scar it leaves as a definition you spend your life
refuting although that hateful word is only a slim line
drawn on a shore and quickly dissolved in a seaworld
any moment when an equally mindless wave fondles it

*like the accidental touch of a finger on a clarinet stop
that the musician converts into silence in order to let the
true note ring out loud.*

Bride read three more pages in quick succession.

*Trying to understand racist malignancy only feeds it,
makes it balloon-fat and lofty floating high overhead
fearful of sinking to earth where a blade of grass could
puncture it letting its watery feces soil the enthralled
audience the way mold ruins piano keys both black and
white, sharp and flat to produce a dirge of its decay.*

*I refuse to be ashamed of my shame, you know, the one
assigned to me which matches the low priority and the
degraded morality of those who insist upon this most
facile of human feelings of inferiority and flaw simply to
disguise their own cowardice by pretending it is identical
to a banjo's purity.*

*Thank you. You showed me rage and frailty and hostile
recklessness and worry worry worry dappled with such
uncompromising shards of light and love it seemed a
kindness in order to be able to leave you and not fold
into a grief so deep it would break not the heart but the
mind that knows the oboe's shriek and the way it tears
into rags of silence to expose your beauty too dazzling*

*to contain and which turns its melody into the grace of
livable space.*

Puzzled, Bride raised her eyes from the pages and looked
at Queen, who said, "Interesting, is it?"

"Very," answered Bride. "But strange too. I wonder who
he was talking to."

"Himself," said Queen. "I bet they're all about him.
Don't you think so?"

"No," murmured Bride. "These are about me, our time
together." Then she read the last page.

*You should take heartbreak of whatever kind seriously
with the courage to let it blaze and burn like the
pulsing star it is unable or unwilling to be soothed into
pathetic self-blame because its explosive brilliance rings
justifiably loud like the din of a tympani.*

Bride put the papers down and covered her eyes.

"Go see him," said Queen, her voice low. "He's down
the road, the last house beside the stream. Come on, get up,
wash your face and go."

"I'm not sure I should, now." Bride shook her head. She
had counted on her looks for so long—how well beauty
worked. She had not known its shallowness or her own
cowardice—the vital lesson Sweetness taught and nailed to
her spine to curve it.

"What's the matter with you?" Queen sounded annoyed. "You come all this way and just turn around and leave?" Then she started singing, imitating the voice of a baby:

Don't know why
There's no sun up in the sky . . .
Can't go on.
Everything I had is gone,
Stormy weather . . .

"Damn!" Bride slapped the table. "You're absolutely right! Totally right! This is about me, not him. Me!"

"You? Get out!" Booker rose from his narrow bed and pointed at Bride, who was standing in the door of his trailer.

"Fuck you! I'm not leaving here until you—"

"I said get out! Now!" Booker's eyes were both dead and alive with hatred. His uncast arm pointed toward the door. Bride ran nine quick steps forward and slapped Booker's face as hard as she could. He hit her back with just enough force to knock her down. Scrambling up, she grabbed a Michelob bottle from a counter and broke it over his head. Booker fell back on his bed, motionless. Tightening her fist on the neck of the broken bottle, Bride stared at the blood seeping into his left ear. A few seconds later he regained consciousness, leaned on his elbow and, with squinty, unfocused eyes, turned to look at her.

"You walked out on me," she screamed. "Without a word! Nothing! Now I want that word. Whatever it is I want to hear it. Now!"

Booker, wiping blood from the left side of his face with his right hand, snarled, "I don't have to tell you shit."

"Oh, yes you do." She raised the broken bottle.

"You get out of my house before something bad happens."

"Shut up and answer me!"

"Jesus, woman."

"Why? I have to know, Booker."

"First tell me why you bought presents for a child molester—in prison for it, for Christ's sake. Tell me why you sucked up to a monster."

"I lied! I lied! I lied! She was innocent. I helped convict her but she didn't do any of that. I wanted to make amends but she beat the crap out of me and I deserved it."

The room temperature had not risen, but Bride was sweating, her forehead, upper lip, even her armpits were soaking.

"You lied? What the hell for?"

"So my mother would hold my hand!"

"What?"

"And look at me with proud eyes, for once."

"So, did she?"

"Yes. She even liked me."

"So you mean to tell me—"

"Shut up and talk! Why did you walk out on me?"

"Oh, God." Booker wiped more blood from the side of his face. "Look. Well, see. My brother, he was murdered by a freak, a predator like the one I thought you were forgiving and—"

"I don't care! I didn't do it! It wasn't me who killed your brother."

"All right! All right! I get that, but—"

"But nothing! I was trying to make up to someone I ruined. You just ran around blaming everybody. You bastard. Here, wipe your bloody hand." Bride threw a dish towel toward him and put down what was left of the bottle. After wiping her palms on her jeans and brushing hair from her damp forehead, she looked steadily at Booker. "You don't have to love me but you damn well have to respect me." She sat down in a chair by the table and crossed her legs.

In a long silence cut only by the sound of their breathing, they stared not at each other but away—at the floor, their hands, through the window. Minutes passed.

At last Booker felt he had something definitive and vital to say, to explain, but when he opened his mouth his tongue froze—the words were not there. No matter. Bride was asleep in the chair, her chin pointing toward her chest, her long legs splayed.

. . .

Queen didn't knock; she simply opened the door to Booker's trailer and stepped in. When she saw Bride sprawled asleep in a chair and the bruise over Booker's eye she said, "Good Lord. What happened?"

"Dustup," said Booker.

"Is she okay?"

"Yeah. Knocked herself out and fell asleep."

"Some 'dustup.' She came all this way to beat you up? For what? Love or misery?"

"Both, probably."

"Well, let's get her out of that chair and on the bed," said Queen.

"Right." Booker stood up. With Queen's help and his one working arm they got her on his narrow, unmade bed. Bride moaned, but did not wake.

Queen sat down at the table. "What you gonna do about her?"

"I don't know," answered Booker. "It was perfect for a while, the two of us."

"What caused the split?"

"Lies. Silence. Just not saying what was true or why."

"About?"

"About us as kids, things that happened, why we did things, thought things, took actions that were really about what went on when we were just children."

"Adam for you?"

"Adam for me."

"And for her?"

"A big lie she told when she was a kid that helped put an innocent woman in prison. A long sentence for child rape the woman never did. I walked out after we quarreled about Bride's strange affection for the woman. At least it seemed strange at the time. I didn't want to be anywhere near her after that."

"What'd she lie for?"

"To get some love—from her mama."

"Lord! What a mess. And you thought about Adam—again. Always Adam."

"Yep."

Queen crossed her wrists and leaned on the table. "How long is he going to run you?"

"I can't help it, Queen."

"No? She told her truth. What's yours?"

Booker didn't answer. The two of them sat in silence with Bride's light snoring the only sound until Queen said, "You need a noble reason to fail, don't you? Or some really deep reason to feel superior."

"Aw, no, Queen. I'm not like that! Not at all."

"Well what? You lash Adam to your shoulders so he can work day and night to fill your brain. Don't you think he's tired? He must be worn out having to die and get no rest because he has to run somebody else's life."

"Adam's not managing me."

"No. You managing him. Did you ever feel free of him? Ever?"

"Well." Booker flashed back to standing in the rain, how his music changed right after he saw Bride stepping into a limousine, how the gloom he had been living in dissipated. He thought about his arms around her waist while they danced and her smile when she turned around. "Well," he repeated, "for a while it was good, really good being with her." He couldn't hide the pleasure in his eyes.

"I guess good isn't good enough for you, so you called Adam back and made his murder turn your brain into a cadaver and your heart's blood formaldehyde."

Booker and Queen stared at each other for a long time until she stood up and, not taking the trouble to hide her disappointment, said, "Fool," and left him slouched in his chair.

Taking her time Queen walked slowly back to her house. Amusement and sadness competed for her attention. She was amused because she hadn't seen lovers fight in decades—not since she lived in the projects in Cleveland where young couples acted out their violent emotions as theatrical performances, aware of a visible or invisible audience. She had experienced it all with multiple husbands, all of whom were now blended into no one. Except her first,

John Loveday, whom she'd divorced—or had she? Hard to remember since she hadn't divorced the next one either. Queen smiled at the selective memory old age blessed her with. But sadness cut through the smile. The anger, the violence on display between Bride and Booker, were unmistakable and typical of the young. Yet, after they hauled the sleeping girl to the bed and laid her down, Queen saw Booker smooth the havoc of Bride's hair away from her forehead. Glancing quickly at his face she was struck by the tenderness in his eyes.

They will blow it, she thought. Each will cling to a sad little story of hurt and sorrow—some long-ago trouble and pain life dumped on their pure and innocent selves. And each one will rewrite that story forever, knowing the plot, guessing the theme, inventing its meaning and dismissing its origin. What waste. She knew from personal experience how hard loving was, how selfish and how easily sundered. Withholding sex or relying on it, ignoring children or devouring them, rerouting true feelings or locking them out. Youth being the excuse for that fortune-cookie love— until it wasn't, until it became pure adult stupidity.

I was pretty once, she thought, real pretty, and I believed it was enough. Well, actually it was until it wasn't, until I had to be a real person, meaning a thinking one. Smart enough to know heavyweight was a condition not a disease; smart enough now to read the minds of selfish people right away. But the smarts came too late for her children.

Each of her "husbands" snatched a child or two from her, claimed them or absconded with them. Some spirited them away to their home countries; another had his mistress capture two; all but one of her husbands—the sweet Johnny Loveday—had good reasons to pretend love: American citizenship, U.S. passport, financial help, nursing care or a temporary home. She had no opportunity to raise a single child beyond the age of twelve. It took some time to figure out the motives for faking love—hers and theirs. Survival, she supposed, literal and emotional. Queen had been through it all, and now she lived alone in the wilderness, knitting and tatting away, grateful that, at last, Sweet Jesus had given her a forgetfulness blanket along with a little pillow of wisdom to comfort her in old age.

Restless and deeply displeased with the turn of events, especially Queen's open disgust with him, Booker went outside and sat on his doorstep. Soon it would be twilight and this haphazard village minus streetlights would disappear in darkness. Music from a few radios would be as distant as the lights flickering from TV sets: old Zeniths and Pioneers. He watched a couple of local trucks rumble by and a few motorcyclists that followed soon after. The truckers wore caps; the motorcyclists wore scarves tied around their foreheads. Booker liked the mild anarchy of the place, its indifference to its residents modified by the presence of his aunt, the single person he trusted. He'd found some on-and-off work with loggers, which was enough until he fell out of a rig and wrecked his shoulder. At every turn, cutting into his aimless thoughts was the picture of the spellbinding black woman lying in his bed, exhausted after screaming and trying her best to kill him or at minimum beat him up. He really didn't know what made her drive all this way except vengeance or outrage—or was it love?

Queen's right, he thought. Except for Adam I don't know anything about love. Adam had no faults, was innocent, pure, easy to love. Had he lived, grown up to have flaws, human failings like deception, foolishness and ignorance, would he be so easy to adore or be even worthy of adoration? What kind of love is it that requires an angel and only an angel for its commitment?

Following that line of thought, Booker continued to chastise himself.

Bride probably knows more about love than I do. At least she's willing to figure it out, do something, risk something and take its measure. I risk nothing. I sit on a throne and identify signs of imperfection in others. I've been charmed by my own intelligence and the moral positions I've taken, along with the insolence that accompanies them. But where is the brilliant research, the enlightening books, the masterpieces I used to dream of producing? Nowhere. Instead I write notes about the shortcomings of others. Easy. So easy.

What about my own? I liked how she looked, fucked, and made no demands. The first major disagreement we had, and I was gone. My only judge being Adam who, as Queen said, is probably weary of being my burden and my cross.

He tiptoed back into his trailer and, listening to Bride's light snoring, retrieved a notebook to once again put on paper words he could not speak.

I don't miss you anymore adam rather i miss the emotion that your dying produced a feeling so strong it defined me while it erased you leaving only your absence for me to live in like the silence of the japanese gong that is more thrilling than whatever sound may follow.

I apologize for enslaving you in order to chain myself to the illusion of control and the cheap seduction of power. No slaveowner could have done it better.

Booker put away his notebook. Dusk enveloped him and he let the warm air calm him while he looked forward to the dawn.

Bride woke in sunshine from a dreamless sleep—deeper than drunkenness, deeper than any she had known. Now having slept so many hours she felt more than rested and free of tension; she felt strong. She didn't get up right away;

instead she remained in Booker's bed, eyes closed, enjoying a fresh vitality and blazing clarity. Having confessed Lula Ann's sins she felt newly born. No longer forced to relive, no, outlive the disdain of her mother and the abandonment of her father. Pulling herself away from reverie she sat up and saw Booker drinking coffee at the pull-down table. He looked pensive rather than hostile. So she joined him, picked a strip of bacon from his plate and ate it. Then she bit into his toast.

"Want more?" Booker asked.

"No. No thanks."

"Coffee? Juice?"

"Well, coffee, maybe."

"Sure."

Bride rubbed her eyelids trying to replay the moments before she fell asleep. The swelling over Booker's left temple helped. "You got me over to your bed with one working arm?"

"I had help," said Booker.

"Who from?"

"Queen."

"God. She must think I'm crazy."

"Doubt it." Booker placed a cup of coffee in front of her. "She's an original. Doesn't recognize crazy."

Bride blew away the coffee's steam. "She showed me the things you mailed her. Pages of your writing. Why did you send them to her?"

"I don't know. Maybe I liked them too much to trash but not enough to carry around. I suppose I wanted them to be in a safe place. Queen keeps everything."

"When I read them I knew they were all about me—right?"

"Oh, yeah." Booker rolled his eyes and heaved a theatrical sigh. "Everything is about you except the whole world and the universe it floats in."

"Would you stop making fun of me? You know what I mean. You wrote them when we were together, right?"

"They're just thoughts, Bride. Thoughts about what I was feeling or feared or, most often, what I truly believed—at the time."

"You still believe heartbreak should burn like a star?"

"I do. But stars can explode, disappear. Besides, what we see when we look at them may no longer be there. Some could have died thousands of years ago and we're just now getting their light. Old information looking like news. Speaking of information, how did you find out where I was?"

"A letter came for you. An overdue bill, I mean, from a music repair shop. The Pawn Palace. So I went there."

"Why?"

"To pay them, idiot. They told me where you might be. This dump of a place, and they had a forwarding address to a Q. Olive."

"You paid my bill then drove all this way to slap my face?"

"Maybe. I didn't plan it, but I have to say it did feel good. Anyway I brought you your horn. Is there more coffee?"

"You got it? My trumpet?"

"Of course. It's fixed too."

"Where is it? At Queen's?"

"In the trunk of my car."

Booker's smile traveled from his lips to his eyes. The joy in his face was infantile. "I love you! Love you!" he shouted and ran out the door down the road toward the Jaguar.

It began slowly, gently, as it often does: shy, unsure of how to proceed, fingering its way, slithering tentatively at first because who knows how it might turn out, then gaining confidence in the ecstasy of air, of sunlight, for there was neither in the weeds where it had curled.

It had been lurking in the yard where Queen Olive had burned bedsprings to destroy the annual nest of bedbugs. Now it traveled quickly, flashing now and then a thin red lick of flame, then dying down for seconds before springing up again stronger, thicker, now that the way and the goal were clear: a tasty length of pine rotting at the trailer's pair of back steps. Then the door, more pine, sweet, soft. Finally there was the joy of sucking delicious embroidered fabric of lace, of silk, of velvet.

By the time Bride and Booker got there, a small cluster of people were standing in front of Queen's house—the jobless, several children and the elderly. Smoke was sneaking from the sills and the door saddle when they broke in. First Booker, then Bride right behind him. They dropped to the floor where smoke was thinnest and crawled to the couch where Queen lay still, seduced into unconsciousness by the smiles of smoke without heat. With his one good arm and Bride's two, their eyes watering and throats coughing, they managed to pull the unconscious woman to the floor and drag her out to the tiny front lawn.

"Further! Come on, further!" shouted one of the men standing there. "The whole place could blow!"

Booker was too intent on forcing air into Queen's mouth to hear him. At last in the distance the sirens of fire truck and ambulance excited the children almost as much as the cartoon beauty of a roaring fire. Suddenly, a spark hiding in Queen's hair burst into flame, devouring the mass of red hair in a blink—just enough time for Bride to pull off her T-shirt and use it to smother the hair fire. When, with stinging, singed palms, she tore away the now sooty, smoking shirt, she grimaced at the sight of a few tufts of hair hard to distinguish from the fast-blistering scalp. All the while, Booker was whispering, "Yeah, yeah. Come on, love, come on, come on, lady." Queen was breathing— at least coughing and spitting, major signs of life. As the ambulance parked, the crowd became bigger and some of the onlookers seemed transfixed—but not at the moaning patient being trundled into the ambulance. They were focused, wide-eyed, on Bride's lovely, plump breasts. However pleased the onlookers were, it was zero compared to Bride's delight. So much so she delayed accepting the blanket the medical technician held toward her—until she saw the look on Booker's face. But it was hard to suppress her glee, even though she was slightly ashamed at dividing her attention between the sad sight of Queen's slide into the back of the ambulance and the magical return of her flawless breasts.

Bride and Booker ran to the Jaguar and followed the ambulance.

Once Queen was admitted, Bride spent the days with her, Booker the nights, three of which passed before Queen opened her eyes. Head bandaged, its contents drugged, she recognized neither of her rescuers. All they were able to do was watch the tubes attached to the patient, one clear as glass turning like a rainforest vine, others thin as telephone wire, all secondary to the white clematis bloom covering the soft gurgle from her lips.

Lines of primary colors bled across the screen above the hospital bed. Transparent bags of what looked like flat Champagne dripped into a vine feeding Queen's flaccid arm. Unable to rise to a bedpan, she had to be scoured, oiled and rewrapped—all of which Bride, not trusting the indifferent hands of the nurse, did herself as tenderly as possible. And she bathed her one section at a time, making sure the lady's body was covered in certain areas before and after cleansing. She left Queen's feet untouched because in the evening when Booker relieved her he insisted, like a daily communicant at Easter, on the duty of assuming that act of devotion. He maintained the pedicure, soaped then rinsed Queen's feet, finally massaging them slowly, rhythmically, with a lotion that smelled like heather. He did the same for Queen's hands, all the time cursing himself for the animosity he had felt during their last conversation.

Neither one spoke during those ablutions and, except for Bride's occasional humming, the quiet served as the balm they both needed. They worked together like a true couple, thinking not of themselves, but of helping somebody else. Sitting among other people in a hospital waiting room with nothing to do but worry was an ordeal. But so was staring helplessly at the patient noting every stir, breath or shift of the prone body. After three days of waiting broken by what acts of comfort they could provide, Queen spoke, her voice a rough, unintelligible croak through the oxygen mask. Then late one evening the oxygen mask was removed and Queen whispered, "Am I going to be all right?"

Booker smiled.

"No question. No question at all." He leaned in and kissed her nose.

Queen licked her dry lips, closed her eyes again and began to snore.

When Bride returned to relieve him and he told her what had happened, they celebrated by eating breakfast together in the hospital cafeteria. Bride ordered cereal, Booker orange juice.

"What about your job?" Booker raised his eyebrows.

"What about it?"

"Just asking, Bride. Breakfast conversation, you know?"

"I don't know about my job and don't care. I'll get another one."

"Oh, yeah?"

"Yeah. And you? Logging forever?"

"Maybe. Maybe not. Loggers move on after they destroy a forest."

"Well, don't worry about me."

"But I do."

"Since when?"

"Since you broke a beer bottle over my head."

"Sorry."

"No kidding. Me too."

They chuckled.

Away from Queen's hospital bed, relieved about her progress and in a fairly relaxed mood, they amused themselves with banter like an old couple.

Suddenly, as though he'd forgotten something, Booker snapped his fingers. Then he reached into his shirt pocket and took out Queen's gold earrings. They had been removed to bandage Queen's head. All this time they had been in a little plastic bag tucked in the drawer of her bedside table.

"Take these," he said. "She prized them and would want you to wear them while she recovers."

Bride touched her earlobes, felt the return of tiny holes and teared up while grinning.

"Let me," said Booker. Carefully he inserted the wires into Bride's lobes, saying, "Good thing she was wearing them when the place caught fire because nothing at all is left. No letters, address book, nothing. All burned. So I called my mother and asked her to get in touch with Queen's kids."

"Can she contact them?" asked Bride swerving her head gently back and forth the better to relish the gold discs. Everything was coming back. Almost everything. Almost.

"Some," Booker replied. "A daughter in Texas, medical student. She'll be easy to find."

Bride stirred her oatmeal, tasted a spoonful, found it cold. "She told me she doesn't see any of them, but they send her money."

"They all hate her for some reason or another. I know she abandoned some of them to marry other men. Lots of other men. And she didn't or couldn't take the kids with her. Their fathers made sure of that."

"I think she loves them though," said Bride. "Their photographs were all over the place."

"Yeah, well the motherfucker who murdered my brother had all his victims' photos in his fucking den."

"Not the same, Booker."

"No?" He looked out the window.

"No. Queen loves her children."

"They don't think so."

"Oh, stop it," said Bride. "No more stupid arguments about who loves who." She pushed the cereal bowl to the center of the table and took a sip of his orange juice. "Come on, hateful. Let's go back and see how she's doing."

Standing on either side of Queen's bed, they were extremely happy to hear her speaking loudly and clearly.

"Hannah? Hannah?" Queen was staring at Bride and breathing hard. "Come here, baby. Hannah?"

"Who's Hannah?" asked Bride.

"Her daughter. The medical student."

"She thinks I'm her daughter? God. Drugs, medicine, I guess. That stuff confuses her."

"Or focuses her," said Booker. He lowered his voice. "There was a thing with Hannah. Rumor in the family was that Queen ignored or dismissed the girl's complaint about her father—the Asian one, I believe, or the Texan. I don't know. Anyway she said he fondled her and Queen refused to believe it. The ice between them never melted."

"It's still on her mind."

"Deeper than her mind." Booker sat in a chair near the foot of Queen's bed listening to her persistent call—a whisper now—for Hannah. "Now I think of it, it explains why she told me to hang on to Adam, to keep him close."

"But Hannah isn't dead."

"In a way she is, at least to her mother. You saw that photo display she had on her wall. Takes up all the space. It's like a roll call. Most of the pictures are of Hannah though—as a baby, a teenager, a high school graduate, winning some prize. More like a memorial than a gallery."

Bride moved behind Booker's chair and began to massage his shoulders. "I thought those photos were of all her children," she said.

"Yeah, some are. But Hannah reigns." He rested his head on Bride's stomach and let the tension he didn't know was in him drift away.

Following a few days of cheer-inspiring recovery, Queen was still confused but talking and eating. Her speech was hard to follow since it seemed to consist of geography—the places she had lived in—and anecdotes addressed to Hannah.

Bride and Booker were pleased with the doctor's assessment: "She's doing much better. Much." They relaxed and began to plan what to do when Queen was released. Get a place where all three were together? A big mobile home? At least until Queen could take care of herself, without delving too closely, they assumed the three of them would live together.

Slowly, slowly their bright plans for the immediate future darkened. The carnival-colored lines on the screen began to wiggle and fall, their sliding punctuated by the music of emergency bells. Booker and Bride took shallow breaths as Queen's blood count dropped and her temperature rose. A vicious hospital-borne virus, as sneaky and evil as the flame that had destroyed her home, was attacking the patient. She thrashed a bit then held her arms raised high, her fingers clawing, reaching over and over for the rungs of a ladder that only she could see. Then all of it stopped.

Twelve hours later Queen was dead. One eye was still open, so Bride doubted the fact. It was Booker who closed it, after which he closed his own.

During the three days waiting until Queen's ashes were ready, they argued over the choice of an urn. Bride wanted something elegant in brass; Booker preferred something environmentally friendly that could be buried and in time enrich the soil. When they discovered there was no grave-yard within thirty-five miles, or a suitable place in the trailer park for her burial, they settled for a cardboard box to hold ashes that would be strewn into the stream. Booker insisted on performing the rites alone while Bride waited in the car. She watched him carefully, anxiously, as he walked away toward the river, holding the carton of ashes in his right elbow and his trumpet dangling from the fingers of his left. These last days, thought Bride, while they were fig-uring out what to do, were congenial because their focus was on a third person they both loved. What would happen now, she wondered, when or if there was just the two of them again? She didn't want to be without him, ever, but if she had to she was certain it would be okay. The future? She would handle it.

Although heartfelt, Booker's ceremony to honor his beloved Queen was awkward: the ashes were lumpy and difficult to toss and his musical tribute, his effort at "Kind of Blue," was off-key and uninspired. He cut it short and, with a sadness he had not felt since Adam's death, threw his trumpet into the gray water as though the trumpet had failed him rather than he had failed it. He watched the horn float for a while then sat down on the grass, resting his forehead in his palm. His thoughts were stark, skeletal. It never occurred to him that Queen would die or even could die. Much of the time, while he tended her feet and listened to her breath he was thinking about his own unease. How disrupted his life had become, what with caring for an aunt he adored and who was now dead due to her own carelessness—who the hell burns bedsprings these days? How acute his predicament had become by the sudden return of a woman he once enjoyed, who had changed from one dimension into three—demanding, perceptive, daring. And what made him think he was a talented trumpet player who could do justice to a burial or that music could be his language of memory, of celebration or the displacement of loss? How long had childhood trauma hurtled him away from the rip and wave of life? His eyes burned but were incapable of weeping.

Queen's remains, touched by a rare welcome breeze, drifted farther and farther down-current. The sky, too sullen to keep its promise of sunlight, sent hot moisture instead. Feeling unbearable loneliness as well as profound regret, Booker stood up and joined Bride in the Jaguar.

Inside the car the quiet was thick, brutal, probably because there were no tears and nothing important to say. Except for one thing and one thing only.

Bride took a deep breath before breaking into the deathly silence. Now or never, she thought.

"I'm pregnant," she said in a clear, calm voice. She looked straight ahead at the well-traveled road of dirt and gravel.

"What did you say?" Booker's voice cracked.

"You heard me. I'm pregnant and it's yours."

Booker gazed at her a long time before looking away toward the river where a smattering of Queen's ashes still floated but the trumpet had disappeared. One by fire, one by water, two of what he had so intensely loved gone, he thought. He couldn't lose a third. With just a hint of a smile he turned around to look again at Bride.

"No," he said. "It's ours."

Then he offered her the hand she had craved all her life, the hand that did not need a lie to deserve it, the hand of trust and caring for—a combination that some call natural love. Bride stroked Booker's palm then threaded her fingers through his. They kissed, lightly, before leaning back on the headrests to let their spines sink into the seats' soft hide of cattle. Staring through the windshield, each of them began to imagine what the future would certainly be.

No lonesome wandering child with a fishing pole passed by and glanced at the adults in the dusty gray car. But if one had, he or she might have noticed the pronounced smiles of the couple, how dreamy their eyes were, but would not care a bit what caused that shine of happiness.

A child. New life. Immune to evil or illness, protected from kidnap, beatings, rape, racism, insult, hurt, self-loathing, abandonment. Error-free. All goodness. Minus wrath.

So they believe.

Sweetness

I prefer this place—Winston House—to those big, expensive nursing homes outside the city. Mine is small, homey, cheaper, with twenty-four-hour nurses and a doctor who comes twice a week. I'm only sixty-three—too young for pasture—but I came down with some creeping bone disease, so good care is vital. The boredom is worse than the weakness or the pain, but the nurses are lovely. One just kissed me on the cheek before congratulating me when I told her I was going to be a grandmother. Her smile and her compliments were fit for someone about to be crowned.

I had showed her the note on blue paper that I got from Lula Ann—well, she signed it "Bride," but I never pay that any attention. Her words sounded giddy. "Guess what, S. I am so so happy to pass along this news. I am going to have a baby. I'm too too thrilled and hope you are too." I reckon the thrill is about the baby, not its father, because she doesn't mention him at all. I wonder if he is as black as she is. If so, she needn't worry like I did. Things have changed a mite from when I was young. Blue blacks are all over TV, in fashion magazines, commercials, even starring in movies.

There is no return address on the envelope. So I guess I'm still the bad parent being punished forever till the day I die for doing the well-intended and, in fact, necessary way I brought her up. I know she hates me. As soon as she could she left me all alone in that awful apartment. She got as far away from me as she could: dolled herself up and got some big-time job in California. The last time I saw her she looked so good, I forgot about her color. Still, our relationship is down to her sending me money. I have to say I'm grateful for the cash because I don't have to beg for extras like some of the other patients. If I want my own fresh deck of cards for solitaire I can get it and not need to play with the dirty, worn one in the lounge. And I can buy my special face cream. But I'm not fooled. I know the money she sends is a way to stay away and quiet down the little bit of conscience she's got left.

If I sound irritable, ungrateful, part of it is because underneath is regret. All the little things I didn't do or did wrong. I remember when she had her first period and how I reacted. Or the times I shouted when she stumbled or dropped something. How I screamed at her to keep her from tattling on the landlord—the dog. True. I was really upset, even repelled by her black skin when she was born and at first I thought of . . . No. I have to push those memories away—fast. No point. I know I did the best for her under the circumstances. When my husband ran out on us, Lula Ann was a burden. A heavy one but I bore it well.

Yes, I was tough on her. You bet I was. After she got all that attention following the trial of those teachers, she became hard to handle. By the time she turned twelve going on thirteen I had to be even tougher. She was talking back, refusing to eat what I cooked, primping her hair. When I braided it, she'd go to school and unbraid it. I couldn't let her go bad. I slammed the lid and warned her of the names she'd be called. Still, some of my schooling must have rubbed off. See how she turned out? A rich career girl. Can you beat it?

Now she's pregnant. Good move, Lula Ann. If you think mothering is all cooing, booties and diapers you're in for a big shock. Big. You and your nameless boyfriend, husband, pickup—whoever—imagine OOOH! A baby! Kitchee kitchee koo!

Listen to me. You are about to find out what it takes, how the world is, how it works and how it changes when you are a parent.

Good luck and God help the child.

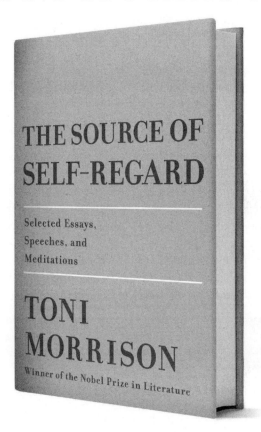

PARADISE

"They shoot the white girl first. With the rest they can take their time." So begins *Paradise*, which opens with a horrifying scene of mass violence and chronicles its genesis in an all-black small town in rural Oklahoma. Founded by the descendants of freed slaves and survivors in exodus from a hostile world, the patriarchal community of Ruby is built on righteousness, rigidly enforced moral law, and fear. But seventeen miles away, another group of exiles has gathered in a promised land of their own. And it is upon these women in flight from death and despair that nine male citizens of Ruby will lay their pain, terror, and murderous rage. In prose that soars with the rhythms, grandeur, and tragic arc of an epic poem, Toni Morrison challenges our most fiercely held beliefs as she weaves folklore and history, memory and myth into an unforgettable meditation on race, religion, gender, and a far-off past that is ever present.

Fiction